STO

MYSTERY

W9-BBD-754

896

DO NOT REMOVE
CARDS FROM POCKET

MAR 1 5 1982

ALLEN COUNTY PUBLIC LIBRARY

FORT WAYNE, INDIANA 46802

You may return this book to any agency, branch,
or bookmobile of the Allen County Public Library

DEMCO

THE
SEVENTH RAVEN

By the same author:

THE WEATHERMONGER

HEARTSEASE

THE DEVIL'S CHILDREN

EMMA TUPPER'S DIARY

THE DANCING BEAR

THE GIFT

THE BLUE HAWK

CHANCE, LUCK AND DESTINY

ANNERTON PIT

TULKU

CITY OF GOLD AND OTHER
STORIES FROM THE OLD TESTAMENT

THE
SEVENTH RAVEN

PETER DICKINSON

A Unicorn Book

E. P. DUTTON   NEW YORK

ALLEN COUNTY PUBLIC LIBRARY
FORT WAYNE, INDIANA

First published in the U.S.A. 1981 by Elsevier-Dutton
Publishing Co., Inc., 2 Park Avenue, New York, N.Y. 10016

Copyright © 1981 by Peter Dickinson

All rights reserved. No part of this publication may be
reproduced or transmitted in any form or by any means,
electronic or mechanical, including photocopy, recording,
or any information storage and retrieval system now
known or to be invented, without permission in writing
from the publisher, except by a reviewer who wishes to
quote brief passages in connection with a review written
for inclusion in a magazine, newspaper, or broadcast.

Library of Congress Cataloging in Publication Data

Dickinson, Peter, date   The seventh raven.
(A Unicorn book.)

Summary: In a bungled attempt to kidnap an ambassador's
son, four revolutionaries make hostages of a hundred
children rehearsing an opera.
[1. Terrorism—Fiction.   2. Amateur theatricals—Fiction]
I. Title.
PZ7.D562Se   1981   [Fic]   81-3213
ISBN 0-525-39150-9   AACR2

Printed in the U.S.A.   First Edition
10 9 8 7 6 5 4 3 2 1

For
Serena Hughes

2147896

2147295

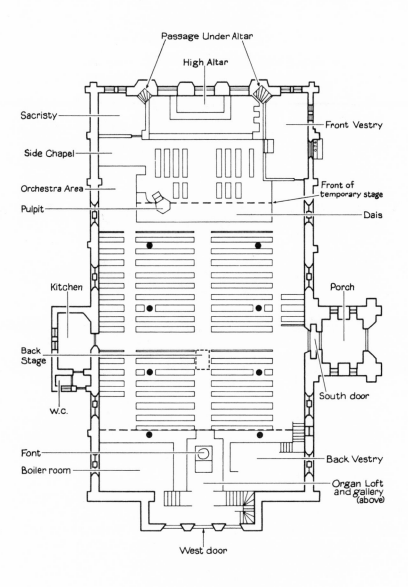

ST ANDREW'S CHURCH, KENSINGTON

Chapter One

When I was nine I was an owl. Next year I was an Egyptian slave. Next I was a rib of the whale that swallowed Jonah. Next I was a flame in the burning fiery furnace that didn't burn Shadrach, Meshach and Abednego. Next I was an Egyptian slave again, but chief slave this time. Then, three years running, I was a wicked woman.

Those were my best years, especially the second one when I was a citizen of the wicked city where the Prodigal Son lost all his money. We did it like jazz-age Chicago and I had a foot-long cigarette holder to smoke and a saxophone wailed away in the pulpit and strobe lights glittered on and off and Mrs Dunnitt as usual had made us fantastic costumes—she always does but that year they weren't just fantastically beautiful, they were fantastically sexy too, and I shan't ever forget the sheer kick of trying out what it was like to feel like that, under all those lights, in front of Mum and Dad and both Grannies and all my friends' families, in a church.

Actually I shan't ever forget any of it. By the time I was doing my wicked-woman parts I could understand what it was all about, and I could think about it as if I were outside it all, as well as being inside. For instance I could tell you what went wrong last year, so that we only just brought it off. But even that first year of all, when I could hardly see a thing out of my owl mask and I was supposed to be watching Toby's baton so that I could squeak *Kyrie Eleison* in time but I had a peacock in front of me with a floppy great tail and I tripped over it at the dress rehearsal and spoilt the whole procession and I couldn't go to sleep because I was so worried about doing it again in front of Granny Tope (Granny Jacobs wouldn't mind, of course, she'd think it was a joke)—even then, though I hardly understood anything that was happening, I knew that this was going to be one of the most important things in my life and I was going to be in it every year, for ever.

Last year, at twenty-five minutes to four on the third of September, Mum said, "Darling, you realise they'll probably decide you're too old for the opera this time?"

"Of course I know," I said.

We'd picked about twenty pounds of runner beans and were sitting on deck-chairs on the lawn behind the cottage, chopping them up for the freezer. Dad was back at his office. Trog—that's my eldest brother—had a job too and had only been down for the odd weekend. Marco—that's my other brother—was cameraman for a team from Cambridge who'd conned some money out of a tobacco company to go and investigate some lakes in the Andes which kept disappearing and coming back again. In theory he'd be home next week, but we hadn't heard from him for yonks. It would be typical of Marco, Dad said, to get himself drowned in a lake which wasn't there.

The holidays had seemed very strange without them, and now only Mum and me were left to freeze the beans and shut the cottage up and hope the Welsh Nationalists wouldn't come and burn it down while we were in London. We probably wouldn't be coming back till April and I could sense that then everything would be different, even if the Nats hadn't done their beastliest. We were going to change, so the way we used the cottage would change too. This—sitting on the lawn chopping the beans—was a kind of last time, and I didn't like it. I was edgy too about getting back to London and finding whether Adam still felt the same about me, and me about him. Letters don't really tell you—certainly Adam's don't. It was a fabulous day, brisk but sunny, smelling of bracken and ripe apples, but even the sunlight seemed to be a colour which showed that summer was almost ended. That and Adam and the cottage were quite enough without Mum bringing up the opera too. I must have sounded really snappy when I answered.

Of course Mum didn't notice. It was quite surprising that she'd got round to thinking at all about me minding being out of the opera. She put her beans down and craned at me, earnest-tortoise. Her great thick specs always make her eyes look misty and sad, though when you see her without them you get quite a shock because really her eyes are small and glinting and you recognise the likeness to Granny Tope—though then Mum can hardly see anything, of course.

"Year after year," she said, "we've vaguely agreed we can't cope with more than a hundred in the cast, and year after year it's been more. Last year was the utter limit. A hundred and seventeen. We made a sort of vow at the post-mortem we wouldn't let it happen again."

"I know all that," I said. "You don't have to go on."

"Yes I do," she said. "It's for my sake as much as yours. You see *we've* got to set the example. We can't enforce an age-limit on the others and make an exception because you're my daughter."

"Do shut up, Mum," I said, "or I'll take Noggin for a walk and leave you with all these bloody beans."

Noggin is our cat and yes, he likes being taken for walks. Three miles is his limit, but however long or short the walk is he knows the moment you turn for home and sits down and miaows and you have to carry him all the way back.

"Provided you understand, darling," said Mum.

"I understand a whole lot more than you realise," I said.

I *think* that's true. Take Mum, for instance—or rather, take Mum and me. Nobody's ever even hinted, but I'm fairly sure she didn't want to have me. Marco's five years older than me, so he'd have been just going off to nursery school when Mum got pregnant with me. Some of my friends are eldests in their families, instead of being youngests like me, so I know how the mums live who've got small children. They're slaves, absolute slaves. The year I was chief slave in the opera, Prue—our producer—told us that to look like a slave you had to think and feel like a slave. She said it would be difficult for us because we didn't know any slaves, but I thought of Mrs Conyers-Smith who had four-year-old twin boys plus a new baby plus Mr Conyers-Smith who expected a pretty wife and a three-course meal when he got home from his office. Prue said afterwards that I must have been a slave in a previous incarnation. I was pleased, but I didn't explain about Mrs Conyers-Smith. I baby-sat once or twice for the twins as a sort of invisible thank-you, but it turned out Mrs Conyers-Smith was the sort who actually thinks it's great being a slave. That's why she and Mr Conyers-Smith chose each other, I suppose.

Anyway, Mum's not like that at all. Being a slave would be hell for her, particularly because there's something else she could have been. I began to realise this my first wicked-woman year—the opera was a rather soppy story about what was happening in the inn while Jesus was being born in the stable but it had gorgeous music, difficult lacy backings and big main tunes we could really bounce along. After the dress rehearsal Mum hauled me off to say hello to an old man who'd been watching. He was small and flabby and smelt disgusting—not dirty, but sickly sweet, like stale marzipan—and he looked at me as if I was some kind of boring animal. He wheezed and stared for a little, and when he spoke he had such a thick accent I could hardly understand what he was saying.

"You have no voice, even," he croaked.

"'Fraid not," I said. It was true, so I didn't mind. I can sing on the note, but that's all. He might have said that I made up for it by being pretty good at being wicked, but by then I'd been around the opera long enough to recognise the types who think the music's all that matters, and everything else is frills. I could see this friend of Mum's was an extreme case. Then he said something I didn't understand at all.

"In that case, young lady, you will need to work very hard in other ways."

"What for?" I said. I was beginning not to like him.

"To have been worth it," he said.

He turned his back on me. I could see Mum was upset, which was unusual. I mean she's often upset, but you don't see it. I didn't want to bother her but next time I was having a piano lesson I asked Mrs Parsons about the man. She doesn't help with the opera but she's Mum's oldest friend. Her daughter Chloe's the same age as me, but we don't get on all that well. Chloe's got an amazing voice so she's had solo parts in the opera almost since she started, but she's as boring as a dishcloth in every other way. I expect she thinks the same about me. Mrs Parsons is large and sort of shapeless. Dad says she needs requilting. She usually waits before she answers even the simplest question, as though it might hold a hidden trap, but she came straight out with what she thought about the smelly old man.

"He's a spiteful little toad," she said.

"Why did Mum ask him along? She can't like him, can she?"

"No, but she can admire him."

"What on earth for?"

"For being a genius, I suppose."

"What at?"

"Teaching."

"Oh—cello. He taught Mum?"

"Let's start at bar fifty, shall we?"

"Isn't what Mr Genius said more important?"

"In the eye of God, I daresay. I'm just your piano teacher."

"Not just. You're Mum's friend."

"Bar fifty."

"Not till you've told me one thing more. I don't know what. Just one useful little thing for me to think about."

Long pause. Sigh.

"That kind of teacher, Doll, is very demanding of his pupils. It's an insult when they want to do anything except be taught by him and play the way he's taught them."

"They must have to be extra good, too."

"That goes without saying."

"Well, thanks. Bar fifty, here I come."

I thought quite a bit about what Mrs Parsons said, and I tied it in with a few other things, especially Mum's Testori. The Testori is Mum's cello. Dad bought it for her when Marco was born. He had to borrow the money, because it cost £3,000 then. It's insured for £70,000 now. She has a couple of other cellos which she calls her rattle-boxes, but the Testori is the sort of cello that gets illustrated in books on musical instruments. Of course I knew that Mum had been a concert cellist when she married Dad, but until Mrs Parsons explained about horrible Mr Genius I hadn't ever thought it was a bit odd Dad giving her something like the Testori *after* she'd stopped her career. Of course, they didn't think she'd stopped it then. The Testori must have been a sort of promise between them that as soon as the boys were a few years old she was going back to it. I don't mean just playing in a professional orchestra. She could still do that, if she wanted to—any of the big orchestras would be glad to have her. I know enough about music to know she's really extra good. But if she hadn't given up when she did she could have been the sort of player people go and listen to because it's her—Elsie Tope— playing, the way they go and listen to Rostropovich because it's him. Perhaps I'm just fantasising. Or perhaps Mum and Dad might have been fantasising too, and actually she mightn't have turned out that good. But what Mr Genius said, and the way he said it—I can see now that he really hated me, not because of what I was like but because I existed at all—makes me think perhaps it's true. There was this other person Mum could have been, a star of stars, making her gorgeous music with the world fighting for tickets. She married Dad and took time off from her career to have the boys, close together, and get them started, and then it would have been possible to go back to Mr Genius. But at the crucial point I came along, the accident. By the time I was old enough somehow or other it was too late—or perhaps I just tipped the balance by making the family big enough to matter more than a career—and Mum had to settle for living her life as just Mum, and playing mostly with friends who aren't in her class, and so on.

Plus, of course, the opera.

That's terribly important. It may seem funny because some years there isn't even a cello part and when there is it may not be very interesting, but it doesn't matter. For Mum—and I suppose in their own ways for Mrs Dunnitt and Mrs Banks and Mr and Mrs Slim (who we usually call the opera mafia)—but for Mum most of all it's as though our ugly black barn of a church was the cello, and the children were the bow, and by putting them together she got them to make this music nobody else could make. I really mean that. I'm not just being insular, but I absolutely bet there isn't anything else quite like our opera in all the world. There must be other things which are even better, but still they can't be like. Somehow or other I knew this when I was a panicky little girl in an owl-mask desperately craning to watch Toby's baton and at the same time trying not to trip over the tail of the stupid peacock in front of me. I suppose that's why I minded so much knowing that this time I couldn't be in it. Of course I'd known, yonks before, but it wasn't until half-way through the afternoon of September the third that I understood what it was going to feel like.

Mum really is rather extraordinary. We had a stupid vile quarrel about the beans because she didn't want to be bothered to freeze them the proper way and I couldn't see the point of sowing them and hoeing them and staking them and picking them and chopping them if we were only going to turn them into slimy green mush in the end. We hardly spoke to each other all evening. Mum went off to bed after the nine o'clock news and I stayed up listening to Adam's favourite records. When I was doing my teeth—about one in the morning, I suppose—and sloshing around and making as much noise as I could without being forced to admit to myself that I was doing it on purpose, I noticed she'd left her Valium on the shelf above the basin. I knew at once she'd done it in case I wanted one. She usually hides it, and doesn't like even Dad to know whether she's been taking it or not. But that night she'd guessed how I was feeling. I don't cry, ever. We're bottlers-up, we Jacobses. But it was touch and go.

I didn't take one of the pills. Instead I solved my problems by deciding that somehow or other I was going to muscle into the opera mafia, and get my kicks that way.

Chapter Two

I lay under Mrs Banks's piano purring over my lists. Not purring aloud, of course, but when I'd been helping Mrs Banks make the coffee she'd flashed her steely quick eyes at me and snapped, "You look like that cat of yours." I'd known her long enough to understand she wasn't accusing me of anything—it's just the way she talks—and I'd laughed because she was so right. Not that she can ever have carried Noggin home from a walk—he purrs the whole way and looks so smug that you know he thinks he's got the world into exactly the shape he wants it, and that was how I felt, that evening, when I'd got myself into the first real mafia meeting as list-maker and coffee-helper.

It had been touch and go whether they'd have me. At the cottage all I'd planned was to hang around all the rehearsals and pick up any little chores that were going until they found I was doing so much they couldn't get on without me; but the first night I was back in London I went round to the Slims to listen to the new stereo outfit Adam had put together, and it had been Mr Slim who let me in.

Mr Slim had his guilty-thing-surprised look, which was quite normal. If he runs the rest of his life the way he runs the opera part, practically everybody who knocks on his door has probably come to remind him about something he promised to do last week. This may be why he usually looks pleased to see me, because he hasn't promised me anything. He and Mrs Slim approve of me almost too much for comfort. Of course anything would be better than Adam's last girl, who was the rudest person I ever met including frightful Mr Genius, but it makes us a bit of a laughing-stock among the rest of our friends that we don't have anything serious by way of parent-trouble.

"Hi, Dave," I said. "Have a good summer?"

"As far as I can remember, Doll. I suppose you want to see Adam?"

"Has he been behaving himself?"

"In what sense?"

That's a problem with people like Mr Slim. You say something banal, just to keep the conversation chugging along, and he takes it as though it had a real meaning. I suppose I wanted to know whether Adam had been going around with strange women, but that wasn't Mr Slim's business. He blinked and rescued me.

"He's earned himself enough money to buy an earthquake-simulator," he said.

"I've come to hear it. It sounds smashing."

"The exact word. By the by, I hear that you're not going to offer us one of your variations on vice this year."

"Too old at seventeen."

He pulled a sad face. His skin looks like dough which you could punch into any shape you wanted. He has short brown hair sticking straight up and doggy dark eyes. He should have been a circus clown, instead of which he does something with foreign currency in a bank. Apparently he's a wizard at it, because Adam says other banks keep trying to lure him away, but the year when Mrs Talati had her miscarriage and the Talatis couldn't look after the opera funds and Mr Slim took over, he made such a mess of them it took Mr Talati two months to sort it all out. Now he looked so sad at the idea of me being too old at seventeen that I said the first thing that came into my head to cheer him up.

"Never mind—I'm going to help like anything behind the scenes."

"Um," he said.

Adam came down the stairs, two at a time but making no noise at all.

"Hi," we said.

I stared at him. He was incredibly brown. I just managed not to ask if he'd got my last three letters.

"My, you've grown," he said.

"I've lost five ounces."

The telephone rang.

"It's for you," said Mr Slim.

Adam shrugged and ran on down to the kitchen.

"Have you talked to Elsie about this?" said Mr Slim.

"No. It wouldn't be fair."

"What do you mean?"

"Using her. I know you don't like hangers-on. I'm just going to worm my way in. Oh, please forget I told you!"

He scratched his nose, the same way Adam does. It's unsettling how parents will suddenly look like their children for an instant and then slip back to being themselves.

"The thing is," said Mr Slim, "the whole machine only just works. Every year it seems a miracle it doesn't fly apart, but it doesn't because we run it as a ruthless oligarchy. Hangers-on aren't just a nuisance because they wear clogs and mutter in rehearsals—in any numbers they would introduce an element of democracy which would make the thing impossible."

"Just me," I said.

"My dear Doll, that's the trouble. If it could be just you . . ."

"Will you ask? Please? You understand about Mum, don't you? She'll say no, but she'll be aching to be outvoted . . ."

I stopped because Adam came up the stairs.

"It was for you," he said. "Apparently you're supposed to be at the Carlton Tower lushing up a gang of Japanese in the Chelsea Bar."

"Oh God!" said Mr Slim. "I thought that was tomorrow!"

"It's today, Dad, but don't worry. You've got forty minutes.
Patricia just rang to check you'd remembered."

"Scoundrel child. All right, Doll—I'll put it to them."

We waited to let him go up the stairs. I wanted to grab Adam
for a good hug but he was muttering to himself.

"Problems?" I said.

"I shouldn't have done that. He had a sort of not-quite heart-
attack in the summer. I keep forgetting."

"That's awful!"

"Not as bad as it sounds, the medics say . . . put what to
who?"

"Ask the opera mafia if I can join them."

"God, Doll! Seriously?"

"Yes."

"But I've been telling myself all summer at least we won't
have that effete irrelevant bourgeois crap in our hair this time!"

I felt ice in my stomach until he grinned.

"Come and listen to my new speakers," he said. "I'll put on
something really heavy to drown my screams of rage."

Slowly the ice went away. We had a good evening listening to
records, talking about what we'd done in the summer, drinking
home-brew lager and eating ryvita and marmite. But it was
extraordinary to have found out that if I'd had to choose
between Adam and the opera I'd have chosen the opera. I
couldn't get over the strangeness of it all the time I was with
him.

Mr Slim must have put it up pretty cunningly. At any rate, there
I was under the piano with my lists. All the solo parts, so many
tribesmen, so many warriors, so many priests of Baal, so many
prophets of Yahweh, so many handmaids for Jezebel, so many
royal slaves, horses for the chariots, goats and donkeys for the
peasants, bulls for the sacrifice, six ravens even to feed Elijah in
the desert. Besides that list I had another of all the children

who'd been to the audition, with scrawls about whether they could sing—most we knew from other years but some were new and some had got better or worse. We'd got as far as the bulls.

"Hattie Tolland for a start," said Mrs Slim. "She's still a hopeless croaker, poor lamb. I don't think the bulls sing, do they? She can be the front legs and we can get rid of another croaker at the back."

"I thought there were supposed to be two bulls," said Mrs Banks. "One for Elijah and one for the Priests of Baal."

"Oh, good. Four croakers, then," said Mrs Slim.

"Two bull costumes," growled Mrs Dunnitt.

"Come apart," said Bill, looking up from the other end of the room where he'd been arguing about the score with Toby.

"Uh?" said somebody.

Bill uncoiled himself and came staggering across the room. He's an enormously tall, thin bloke, only about twenty-five. He'd written two of our best operas, words and music, and we were doing another of his this time. He always walks as though he was on the point of tripping over something and going sprawling. He talks rather like that too.

"They chopemup and layemon the altars," he said.

"I see," said Mrs Dunnitt icily. "I am to make two bull costumes which will come apart and then go back together for the next performance."

"Spouting blood," said Bill. "Blood everywhere."

"Not on Onward's new carpet," said Mrs Banks.

(I'd been a bit amazed to find that even Mrs Banks called the Rev McIntosh Onward. All the children do, of course. There's never been such a Christian soldier.)

"Terriblydramatic don'tyouthink?" said Bill. "Doyouknow, Passover, Herodstime, wholetemplecourtyard sixinches deepin-blood? Someone's donethesums."

"I will provide two dismemberable costumes," said Mrs Dunnitt as though she were speaking to a thick, deaf foreigner.

"There will be no blood. Mr Tolland will have to do something with the lights."

Bill mumbled disappointedly but shambled away.

"Four croakers, then," said Mrs Slim. "Hattie and Simone and Melissa Tonks and that Jones boy?"

"I didn't realise we'd got a boy left," said Prue. "I can't spare him, even if he's a croaker. Put him among the tribesmen, and let's have a girl dismembered."

Prue Wimbush isn't really one of the mafia. She's more like Toby—I mean she's a professional drama-teacher who does things like our opera for practice and a tiny fee. But she comes to most of the mafia meetings, of course. I looked down my audition list.

"We've got seven boys left," I said. "Three croakers, one squeaker, one whisperer and the Conyers-Smith twins."

"The tribesmen have got some fairly tricky singing," said Mrs Slim.

Mum made agreeing mutters. Those two are the musical conscience. Prue's much more interested in what it all looks like. The funny thing is that Toby, who's supposed to be in charge of the music, often takes Prue's side, but this time Prue gave in.

"Melissa's not really a croaker," said Mum. "Only at auditions. When she's got the others to sing along with she makes quite a good noise."

"Camilla, then?" suggested Mum.

"Camilla Talati or Camilla Fearon?" said Mrs Slim.

"Camilla Talati's a Priest of Baal, isn't she?" said Mum. "And there's a new Camilla, plain as porridge but a good big voice. Drat it, I've lost her."

"Camilla Richardson," I said.

Waiting for the names of the four half-bulls I found myself remembering Adam singing "May I return . . ." in *Joseph and his Amazing Multicoloured Dreamcoat*. Four years before, my chief-slave year. I hadn't liked Adam then. He was a rough, and the only good thing about giving him a big part was that he had less time to spend beating up the other roughs in the back pews during rehearsals; but he'd had a real choir-boy voice, cold and pure as snow. Toby kept trying to get him to coarsen it up, put some blood into it, but Adam paid no attention at all until the actual performances, when suddenly he started coming out with exactly the sort of street-singer noises Toby'd been begging for —perhaps it was the audience, or perhaps it was just the start of his voice breaking. I remembered him alone under the spotlights singing that last song, and how his eyes glittered. Even waiting at the back of the church to lead my slaves up for the final shoutabout—we don't have a final curtain, of course—even from that distance I could feel his triumph and excitement. I wasn't the slightest bit jealous of him being the centre of it all. I forgot he was a rough and I didn't like him . . .

I had to stop day-dreaming and write down the names of the four half-bulls.

"Where does that get us to, Doll?" said Mrs Slim.

There were six empty lines on my last sheet.

"Ninety-four," I said.

"And six ravens to go and that's the lot," said Mum.

They all sighed with happiness at the idea of the sum coming out. The trouble started when they tried to agree on those last six names. I had thirty-one possibles left on my audition list. Twenty-five broken hearts Mrs Slim said. Melissa Tonks was in because she would have been a half-bull if she'd been a worse singer, and it didn't seem fair to leave her out. The new Camilla —Camilla Richardson—because Mum said she was going to be useful in a couple of years time. Katie Drew . . .

"We *ought* to," said Mum with a sigh. "Younger sister, I mean."

"If only Veronica wasn't such a pest," said Mrs Slim.

"At least she can sing," said Mum. "Poor Katie hardly whispered."

"It's that mother of theirs," said Mrs Banks.

"Is that the woman who looks like an Edwardian barmaid?" said Mrs Dunnitt. "Wearing silver fox—genuine, I think."

"Didn't you recognise her?" said Mrs Slim.

"Why should I?" said Mrs Dunnitt.

We all laughed.

"My dear Nancy," said Mum.

"Oh, I remember," said Mrs Dunnitt. "The mother is some sort of television actress, isn't she? I don't have a television, you see. But she's going to help with Veronica's dress this year. She says."

"Another reason for having Katie in," said Mrs Slim. "Anyway, I think she's rather sweet."

I wrote her name down. That left three. They argued around for a while and then changed tack and tried to agree on who shouldn't be in.

"The Conyers-Smith twins for a start," said Mrs Banks.

"They're under age anyway," said Mum.

"In that case what on earth is the woman about, sending them along?" snapped Mrs Banks.

"She told me," said Mrs Slim. "She's hoping to be free for pottery classes on Mondays."

"Honestly, what some of these parents think the opera is *for!*" said Mrs Banks.

Pencils scratched.

"Um?" said Bill, above our heads. I hadn't noticed him coming over. "Did someone say twins? Um, er, identical?"

"Indistinguishable and equally awful," said Mrs Banks.

"Got to have them. Um. I mean, please."

"Why on earth?"

"Got an idea. Terriblydramatic. Next year, you know. This time, um, *blood* them."

There was a long silence, then Mrs Banks said, "If you *must*." I wrote the Conyers-Smith twins down into spaces ninety-eight and ninety-nine. I expect we were just exhausted with arguing.

"One more," said Mrs Slim. "Any candidates . . . ?"

"Let's take a pin," said Mum.

So that's what they did. The lucky tot was somebody called Elizabeth Windsor. I had her voice down as "OK (?)" but nobody could remember what she looked like. Still she was in. The room filled with the shuffling-together of papers and the snap of elastic bands round notebooks.

"Thank the Lord for that," said Mrs Banks. "And do we all solemnly swear that under no circumstances whatsoever will any of us attempt to infiltrate one more ghastly brat into the cast?"

Most of them muttered a sort of yes.

"More coffee, then?" said Mrs Banks.

"I'll get it," I said, wriggling out from the piano. "You needn't come, honestly."

When I got into the hall the door-bell was trying to ring but only making a sputtering noise. I could see the shape of the caller through the frosted glass, so I opened the door. It was Dad.

I was amazed. Dad puts up with the opera for Mum's sake, and mine, but secretly he wishes it didn't happen because it means three months' chaos round our lives each winter. Lots of the husbands feel like that—when the Steinbecks split up two years ago everyone said the opera had been the final straw. Anyway, I didn't expect to see Dad within ten miles of a mafia meeting.

"Hello, Dodo," he said. "Still in session?"

"Just finished. One hundred in the cast exactly. So you're too late if you've come about this other family of yours you've been keeping from us all these years."

He shook his head and sucked in his breath as if I'd told him terrible news, then poked his head round the drawing-room door. I heard the noises of surprise as I went down to get the coffee.

It's funny how you can walk into a room and feel, before you've even looked at the faces, that somebody's angry. It's as strong as the smell of burning. I backed into the drawing-room because I was holding the jugs, but I knew before I turned round. They were all sitting where they'd been, looking at Dad, who was leaning against the piano, serious but a bit bewildered. Even Mr Slim had stopped fiddling with his model stage and was watching him.

". . . didn't realise it was a matter of principle," Dad was saying. "You had getting on for a hundred and twenty last year, I think Elsie told me."

"That's the point," said Mrs Banks. "We made it a principle because of that, and I don't see why we should be expected to go back on it just to make some Whitehall mandarin's job a bit more comfy."

"Oh, I quite agree," said Dad. "Mandarins should be forced to sweat at least once a week. If it was only him . . . but I gather there are several thousand people in the prison camps who might . . ."

"Oh, come!" snorted Mrs Banks.

(That's a funny thing about the opera. Mrs Banks is incredibly far right in politics and probably doesn't believe that anyone except the Russians puts people in prison camps, while Mrs Dunnitt is just as far left and goes and waves banners at demos and stands bail for anarchists. But when it comes to opera politics they are almost Siamese twins.)

"What's it got to do with you, Tony?" said Mr Slim.

Dad relaxed a bit. It might have been just the relief of involving another man in the argument, but Mr Slim is a famous settler of squabbles and unruffler of plumage.

"Good point," said Dad. "My ministry has very little to do with the Foreign Office and my own department nothing at all, but the head of the South American Bureau rang me personally. That means the FO are taking the thing seriously enough to find out what connections they had with you."

"My God!" said Mr Slim.

"Take it easy, darling," said Mrs Slim.

"Don't worry. Only I've just remembered Patricia left a note on my desk asking me to call some fellow at the FO."

"Do you realise," said Mrs Dunnitt, "this means they must have been tapping our phones and opening our mail for weeks? Does anyone seriously think they ought to be allowed to get away with it? Let alone that we should put ourselves out one millimetre for this revolting fascist regime. I know all about them. I was on a vigil outside their embassy only last June. Amnesty have a file three feet thick about their camps and prisons."

"Exactly," said Dad, smooth as hand-lotion. "That's what the chap who rang me chose to stress. If Nancy's right and we've all been under surveillance—though personally I'd say this exchange has become too erratic to be susceptible to tapping —I keep getting that florist's when I try to ring home . . ."

"Stick to the point, darling," said Mum.

"Sorry. What I was told was this. For one reason and another the Foreign Office has decided the time is now ripe to put pressure on the Mattean authorities to do something about their political prisoners. President Blick is definitely dying of cancer. His successor is almost certain to be one Colonel Vanqui, who is something of an Anglophile, and therefore in the opinion of the FO more susceptible than Blick to British opinion. The Mattean ambassador to Great Britain is a nonentity, and owes his appointment to the fact that his wife is Colonel Vanqui's sister. She seems to be a rather formidable lady—indeed, from what my informant said it struck me that some of you might recognise her as a kindred spirit. Be that as it may, the FO are prepared to go to some lengths to retain her good opinion of this country, and since she has set her heart on her son taking part in the opera—she brought him last year and was greatly im-pressed, according to the Mattean cultural attaché who made the original contact—the FO would like to see her wishes respected. It was even hinted to me that if she were to become involved in the opera herself to some extent, there would be an opportunity

for you to put over to her the average British housewife's
feelings about Matteo."

Mrs Dunnitt snorted like a horse. Mrs Banks choked on her
coffee.

"I suppose we could take the Windsor child out," said Mrs
Slim. "We did only choose her with a pin."

I could feel the room bristle.

"Um . . ." said Bill. "If youdothat . . . I'dhaveto . . .
withdraw my opera."

"Hear hear," said Mrs Dunnitt.

"Do I take it," said Dad, "that if the ambassador's son is
included in the cast you are not going to permit your work to be
performed?"

Bill's mouth fell open. I could see Dad scared him. Dad often
sounds like a judge passing sentence—some of my friends can't
do anything but stammer when he's around.

"Oh, er," said Bill. "Not thatatall. Just the, um otherkid. She
was *chosen*, don'tyousee?"

"With a pin," said Dad.

"Yes," said Bill, just as if Dad was agreeing with him that that
was the most important thing. "But, um, sorry . . . my fault . . .
Beginningtothink . . . ought to be *seven* ravens."

"You told us six," said Mum and Mrs Banks and Mrs Slim all
together.

"Terriblysorry," said Bill. "Stupid. Must be seven. See it
now."

"Oh, well," said Mrs Slim in her saddest voice. "One more
year and we've gone over the magic number. Anyone know the
child's name?"

"I don't imagine he troubled to attend the audition," said Mrs
Dunnitt. "He'll appear at the first performance expecting a star
part."

"His name, believe it or not, is O'Grady," said Dad.
"Apparently an Irish adventurer fought in the liberating armies
and left numerous descendants."

"Juan O'Grady," I said. "He came. A hopeless croaker."

"Ravens are supposed to croak," said Bill.

I was still furious. I certainly wasn't going to spoil my lovely list, ending so neatly on the hundredth name, by squeezing another one in at the bottom, so I took a fresh sheet of paper and wrote at the top "Juan O'Grady. Seventh Raven."

Chapter Three

"I'm One," he said (at least I thought he said). "If you call me Jew Ann you get hit."

The main flood of children were streaming in. Already the church was throbbing with the clamour of them.

"One who?"

"One O'Grady."

"You're a raven. Go and wait by the pillar marked D. Next? Boudicca, you're half a bull, pillar C. Liz, you're a priest of Baal, front vestry. Dinah, you're Queen Jezebel . . ."

"Terrific. That's what I wanted. Over at Mrs Banks's?"

"No. Bill's going to tell us about the opera first. Pillar A. Next? What's your name?"

"Queenie," said the child, fat and solemn.

"Uh?"

(I'd learnt my lists by heart. We'd always wasted half the first rehearsal sorting the kids out while the mafia muddled their way through sheets of paper. There wasn't going to be any of that this year. I'd show them. Anyway, I knew there wasn't a Queenie, but sometimes the small ones don't realise they haven't been chosen and come along anyway.)

"You've probably got Elizabeth Windsor," said the child patiently.

"Oh yes. Raven. Pillar D. Melissa, you're Jezebel's handmaid. So are you, Veronica. Pillar A. Tom, soldier, pillar B. Kitty, tribesman, pillar B . . ."

"Do I have to wear a beard *again*?"

"Looks like it. Martin . . ."

The flood began to dwindle. There were gaps. In one of them it struck me out of the blue why the child was called Queenie. Then Tristan Pierce came barging between the swing doors pushing a gleaming new bike.

"Bikes in the porch," I said.

"Not on your nellie. Cost me two hundred quid."

"Bikes in the porch."

He wheeled the thing straight past me and leaned it against the back pews. I was furious. Bikes are a problem—there's not really room in the porch, and expensive ones tend to get clobbered by other kids carelessly hauling their old rattlers out. One year a gang of yobbos hung around and pinched lights and things. Still, it was an absolute rule, no bikes or skateboards in the church, and Tristan knew it as well as I did. I was turning to bawl him out when I saw another bike-wheel nosing through.

"Bikes in the porch," I snarled.

"But Tristan . . ."

"He isn't."

I swung round and saw Mrs Banks was already there, looking beaky and fragile, like some kind of all-wise alien out of Star Trek. Tristan was quite a bit bigger than her, but I could see she was winning. He turned his bike and wheeled it grimly out. Mrs Banks came over.

"Sorry," I began. "I did . . ."

"You're doing wonders, Doll."

"How . . ."

"I told him that if he couldn't keep the rules he couldn't have a part."

"But . . ."

"No prima donnas, no matter what. What on earth . . . ?"

She dashed off in the direction of pillar D. Tristan came in again and swaggered past as if I hadn't been there. I had to call to him where to go. I wondered if he knew how badly we needed him. We were having to use a girl—Sue Ramsay—for Elisha as it was, but Elijah and Ahab absolutely had to be boys, and that meant Jake Laver and Tristan. If either of them fell out we'd have to import someone.

The church was clanging like the inside of a bell. It's a great empty shell of a place, with horrible acoustics until you've got all the pews full. Every mutter becomes an echo, and by now the early arrivals had grown restless and were either beating each other up or shrilling school chatter between the groups into which I'd split them, while some of the smalls were so caught up in the sheer excitement that they had to work it off by running races round the side aisles or worming along the clattery kneelers beneath the pews. The racket round pillar D seemed something extra, though, until Mrs Banks got there and it stilled a little. Mrs Slim came fluttering along the cross-aisle, her hair standing out in a grey frizz all round her smooth brown face.

"Can we start, Doll?" she said. "Are they all in?"

"Fourteen to come, including Jake Laver," I told her.

"Blast him. I wish he wasn't so good at football."

"It'll be better when the evenings get shorter," I said.

Mrs Banks came back and Mrs Slim turned to her.

"We *must* start, Vi. Toby's got to go at seven-ten."

"Somebody's going to have to take special charge of those ravens," said Mrs Banks.

"I knew we shouldn't have had the twins," said Mrs Slim.

"They're nothing to that O'Grady child. Dear Doll, would you . . . ?"

"Who on earth is that *man*?"

"No idea. Look, Toby's waving like a maniac. Doll, you'd better stay with the ravens right through, or we won't get . . ."

"And on your way find out who that *man* is and turf him out. Coming! Coming!"

Mum, who plays the piano for rehearsals, banged a great discord. Toby shrilled his football whistle. Between them they just pierced the clamour and the church hushed.

"Thank you, my dears," said Toby, almost whispering. He's

a squashy round muffin of a man. His main job is running an early-music orchestra and he's getting quite famous for that, but he comes back to conduct our opera every year, for almost nothing. He's done it from the very start. He's vital, because he's the only person who could get those noises out of the children. They'd do anything for him, except keep quiet for more than a few minutes at a time. I tiptoed across to where a man was sitting in the pew just beyond pillar D, and slid in beside him.

"Excuse me," I whispered.

He smiled. He was quite handsome in a synthetic kind of way. Brown skin, shiny black hair, black gaucho moustache, teeth white as paper, sleepy dark eyes.

"Ferdy," he murmured and held out his hand.

I shook it automatically, not feeling as stupid as I might have with anyone else. He was so obviously foreign. He carried his foreignness with him like a kind of private world—as soon as you got inside it you had to follow the customs of *his* country, not yours.

"I'm Doll," I whispered. "Look, I'm sorry, but . . ."

He held up a hand to stop me, then clicked his fingers. There was a rattle and a thud and Juan O'Grady bounced into the pew.

"Hi," he yelled.

I put my finger to my lips. Ferdy whispered in Spanish to Juan.

"Oh, yes . . ." began Juan, still as if he wanted the whole church to know.

Ferdy made a warning hiss, and at once Juan lowered his voice.

"He is my bodyguard," he said. "He has a gun, and if you do not do what I want he will shoot you."

He had no accent, not even an American one, but his English was a little too neat to be real.

"OK," I said. "And if you don't do what we want, such as keeping quiet when Toby and the others are talking, you get turfed out. Right?"

"Then there will be war."

"Makes no difference."

"When I am President, women will not speak to men unless the men command it."

Before I could answer he turned to Ferdy and spoke in Spanish, translating what he'd just said, I guessed. He was a handsome kid, black brows, bright blue eyes and a dreamy complexion. Clearly he thought he was the cat's whiskers.

"When do we *sing*?" he said.

"Ssh. Later. Go back and listen to Toby."

He bounced away. Ferdy smiled at me and shrugged apologetically. Then, quite without warning, he changed. His face didn't move, that I could see, apart from a sort of hardening of the lips and something different around the eyes, but . . . It was a bit like meeting a tiger, I suppose—the suddenness, the hunger, the danger. I don't think Ferdy did it on purpose—it was probably an automatic reaction, on meeting any girl. I didn't swoon, or anything. My first thought was thank God Adam hasn't learnt how to do that.

"Will you be coming to all the rehearsals?" I said.

"Oh, yes," purred the tiger.

"Good," I said.

I was only thinking he might be some help keeping Juan and the twins apart, so I dare say I sounded a bit more businesslike than he'd have expected if the conversation had been going the way he thought it was. Anyway he looked baffled and stopped being a tiger. I pretended to be listening to Toby while I tried to decide whether I'd be pushing my new mafia status a bit too much if I roped this bloke in—it seemed a pity to have him there all the time and not use him. Toby was saying the usual things—about the difference between singing and shouting, about coming to rehearsals and learning the music until they can sing it in their sleep, and so on—but he always manages to make it sound interesting. He finished with a joke. The laughter turned itself into the old, awful clamour. I remembered that Mr

Slim spoke Spanish so I stood on the pew to see if he'd arrived from his office yet so that he could talk to Ferdy about controlling the ravens, but before I spotted him Mum banged the piano and Toby blasted his whistle and Bill, who'd been wandering round the aisles looking lost and miserable, staggered up onto the stage and held up his arms just as if the children had been a rebel army storming his palace and he was surrendering. Silence.

"Um . . ." he said, and turned away, pacing to and fro and muttering to himself. The children watched him as though he was the most interesting thing they'd ever seen. At last he swung and faced them again.

"Imagine this man," he said. "Ordinary man, doing his best, only he happens to be a king. Ahab. That's him—Ahab, King of Israel. Not at all bad at the king job, either. Brave and clever. Fights wars, wins battles, wants peace and quiet. Don't we all? OK, he sits on a gold throne or he drives off to his battles in a gold chariot, and if he doesn't like the look of your face he can have your head cut off, but he's ordinary, ordinary, ordinary. Doing his best at his job. He's easy to imagine, uh? Might be you, might be me, might be Toby, might be anybody. OK? But now you're going to have to stretch your minds a bit, because you're going to have to imagine two extraordinary people. A man and a woman. Elijah's the man and Jezebel's the woman and they're enemies. Total, dead, sworn, never-give-in enemies. Nothing they won't do, nothing on this earth, to beat the other one down. And poor old Ahab, he's their battle-ground. Because he's king, you see?

"Let's take Jezebel first. She's Ahab's chief wife—he's got lots of other wives, but she's the one who counts. Now, she's a foreigner, daughter of the King of Sidon, and she's brought her own god with her to Israel. God called Baal. He's a foreign God and a nasty sort of God and Jezebel won't be happy until everybody in Israel's worshipping her Baal. That's her target, one hundred per cent Baal-worship, and she'll stop at nothing to reach it. She may look soft and glamorous, but really she's as tough as they come. Her idea is to make Ahab send his soldiers through the country killing all the priests and prophets of Yahweh, who's God of Israel. And when Ahab won't do what she wants she forges his name on the orders and gets it done anyway. Poor old ordinary Ahab. Who'd be a king, having to marry a wife like that?

"Why doesn't he give in and get it done with, you might ask. Because of Elijah, that's why. Elijah, the last living prophet of Yahweh. You wouldn't like Elijah if you met him—you'd think he was a perfectly frightful old Ayatollah, thirsting for blood and vengeance. But Elijah is Yahweh's prophet and Yahweh is Ahab's God. Elijah uses that to fight Jezebel. Poor old Ahab—to and fro they battle over him. Now Jezebel's winning and Elijah's flying for his life, hiding in caves, being fed by ravens. Now Elijah's winning and the Israelites are tearing Jezebel's priests to pieces on Mount Carmel. And between them is Ahab, ordinary bourgeois Ahab, longing for peace and quiet, doing his best. Right?

"I've written two sorts of music, one for each side, and before I tell you the actual story, Toby's going to teach you the Yahweh shout and the Baal shout. When Jezebel's winning the Baal music's very fierce and loud and you can hardly hear the Yahweh music at all, and the other way round when Elijah's winning. And there's a third kind of music. Mostly you'll only hear it if you listen carefully, but it's there almost all the time. I call it the Ahab music, but it's more than that. It's the music of all the people who live in Israel, with their sons being taken off for the wars and their crops and animals seized to feed the armies and their fields withering in the drought Yahweh has sent and their babies dying of starvation. It's the music you hear whenever people fight for ideas that seem to them so important that the lives of ordinary people don't matter any more . . . um . . . the still, sad music of humanity . . . sorry.

"Hold it! What Toby was saying about shouting and singing.

I've called these things shouts, but that doesn't mean I don't want them *sung*. Loud as you can, but sung. On the note . . . Thank you."

He stumbled away with his head between his hands as though he'd done something utterly shameful. Toby pranced round checking that the children were in the pews where he wanted them for singing purposes. I whisked the ravens up to their place, right in front on the Yahweh side. I was going to stay with them, though there wasn't really room; but I spotted Mr Slim coming in through the south door and I thought they couldn't really get up to much, right under Toby's nose, so I decided to go and ask him to talk to Ferdy. As I was going down the aisle Ferdy beckoned. I couldn't quite pretend not to see, and if I really wanted him to help . . .

"Excuse," he said. "This historia I know. Is not for the kids, I think?"

"No, not *for* them. *By* them, but *for* adults."

He looked baffled, of course. It's tricky enough explaining to an Englishman that the opera's only a children's opera because it's acted by children, but it's not much use bringing tots along and expecting them to have the time of their lives. Before I could explain, Toby blew his whistle. Mum gave him a note on the piano, and he sang the Yahweh shout. He has a high, wobbly tenor at the best of times, and the shout didn't sound like anything at all, except that the rhythm was peculiar. The Yahweh children copied him when he told them but got it all wrong. He tried several times, but even when they'd got it roughly right it still sounded a mess—or rather it sounded like the kind of music you'd expect Bill to write, full of ums and sorrys.

The Baal shout was easier. The children picked it up almost at once, but they kept trying to smooth the rhythm out and put the beat where you'd expect it and not where Bill wanted it.

"Right," said Toby. "Now you're going to fight it out. Sing, remember. Your weapons are notes of music, not yells. And watch me. If you don't come in bang on time and stop bang on time, to a millionth of a second, it's no good. Off we go. Elsie! Two, three . . . No, no, no! Lousy! Your mouths must be made of wet newspaper. Come on. Greey-yate! Yah-weh! Like that. Two, three . . ."

It was total chaos. He stopped them again and again. He clowned at them, squealed at them, made them sing one note over and over, made them sing pew by pew . . . and then, fabulously, out of the mush of noise I got a glimmer of what Bill was trying to do. Toby caught the moment, whipped the children along and there it was, not a rabble of kids struggling with difficult music in a cold church, but a kind of mad anger, living its own life, bursting out of nowhere, made of music. I could hear—feel—them all grasp what they were doing, as if they had suddenly understood the rules of a new game, and exult in it. My spine tingled with the old joy. It had begun. It was going to work.

I stood up and looked across the church. Mum was lit by the glimmer from her score. She seemed to shine. She was concentrated, frowning, hammering away at the keys, but just as if I'd been right inside her skin I could feel her happiness and share in it. This was what everything else was for.

The ravens ruined it. Toby stopped conducting and dashed across to the front of the Yahweh pews making werewolf claws of his raised hands. The children tried to keep going without him, but within a couple of bars the noise was all loud mush once more and died away, leaving just the whinge of children accusing each other round the raven pew. I heard Ferdy beside me making a click of disapproval with his tongue.

"Stupid," he said. "When the music becoming good."

Toby hoicked a child—I couldn't see who—off the pew, and shoved him down onto the dais steps. He went back to his music-stand shaking his head.

"Well, that wasn't too dusty," he said mildly. "Get that into your heads and we've made a start. Mind you, that's the easiest bit. You're going to have to learn all sorts of tricks with it as we go along. You're really going to have to stretch your teeny talents. OK, Bill's going to tell you the horrible bloodthirsty story of Elijah's battle with Jezebel while I have a bit of a rest. Oh, for heaven's sake! Is anyone supposed to be in charge of these brats in the front row here?"

"Who *was* that man, Doll?" said Mrs Banks. "I noticed you getting quite friendly with him."

I felt myself beginning to blush and felt stupid. The mafia was in session after that first rehearsal—Prue and Bill and Mr Slim on the long sofa arguing about whether Elijah had to have a real fiery chariot to take him up to heaven, and the rest of us round the fire—Mrs Banks always has a log fire, though it's supposed to be a smokeless zone—except for Toby who'd gone off to conduct something at the BBC.

"He's Juan O'Grady's bodyguard," I said.

"Has it come to this?" said Mrs Dunnitt.

"I wish he'd guard him a bit better," said Mrs Banks. "Did you see him fighting that other brat—while Toby was actually conducting? We've never had that before."

"It was the twins' fault," said Mrs Slim. "I saw. One of them was needling him, and then pretending it had been the other one."

"They're incredibly alike, aren't they?" said Mum.

"But actually fighting while Toby . . ." said Mrs Banks.

"I suppose it's the Irish in him . . ." said Mrs Slim.

"I thought Doll was . . ." said Mrs Banks.

"I'm sorry," I said. "I thought they'd be all right if I put them right in front. But . . . actually, the twins are beyond me. I used to baby-sit for Mrs Conyers-Smith when they were smaller. I couldn't cope with them even then."

"Let's turf them out," said Mrs Banks. "And the O'Grady infant, too."

"I had a pathetic telephone call from Mrs Conyers-Smith," said Mrs Slim. "About her pottery class, you know?"

"Oh, Kitty!" said Mrs Banks.

"I didn't promise her anything, of course," said Mrs Slim, shiftily. I could see it all, even the twins being on their worst behaviour that evening because they weren't going to let their Mum get away with wanting to do anything except look after them. I could just imagine her begging them to be good so that she could go and puddle about making ugly thick mugs. I looked at Mum. She was sitting very straight with her lips moving slightly, trying to swallow down the fury she could never let out—fury with Mrs Conyers-Smith, with Mrs Slim, with us, with anyone or anything that might prevent the opera being as good as it possibly could be.

"Doesn't Dave speak Spanish?" I said quickly.

"Dave?" said Mrs Slim, grabbing at the change of subject. "Why yes, of course."

"I thought we might ask Ferdy—that's the bodyguard —to help keep the ravens quiet. Juan think's he's terrific, you know, and he will be coming to all the rehearsals, he told me . . ."

"You realise he's nearly certainly a member of the PDS?" said Mrs Dunnitt.

"Come again?" said Mrs Slim.

"The Matteo political police. Among other things they are responsible for the camps and the torture-houses."

I should have described Mrs Dunnitt earlier. She's quite a bit older than the others. She almost always wears thick tweed jackets and skirts and heavy shoes. Her face is brown, like an old gipsy's, with grey hair pulled hard back and then plaited and coiled into a flat bun. I think the church is the only place I've ever seen her without a cigarette in her mouth. Her voice is dry and croaky at the best of times, but she'd made it drier still now.

"Let's give it another week," said Mrs Slim. "I mean, this *was* the first rehearsal—they might settle down. If Doll could have a word with them, perhaps . . . And if that doesn't work, Nancy,

we're either going to have to ask this man to take charge of them
or else turf them out."

"We really can't have them holding things up," said Mum.
"It's going to be touch and go in any case. I don't know if
you've looked at Bill's score carefully yet . . ."

Mrs Slim made an agreeing worry-mutter. I'd only had a
skim through but even I could see that some of what Bill had
written was almost impossibly tricky. Still, we had to wait for
Mrs Dunnitt. She blew out a long plume of smoke and threw
her unfinished fag into the fire.

"There's a woman called Pettifer . . ." she said.

We relaxed.

"Lady Phoebe Pettifer," said Mrs Banks. I couldn't tell
whether she was happy that Mrs Dunnitt had given in, or just
happy with the title. "New. Her daughter's a tribesman, isn't
she, Doll?"

"She telephoned," said Mrs Dunnitt. "She claims to make
costume jewellery."

"That might be useful," said Mrs Banks.

"If . . ." said Mrs Dunnitt.

That was always the point. If Lady Thing had grasped what
the opera was, she might be marvellous. If not, she'd be a
disaster. I stopped listening and began to try and work out how
on earth I was going to "have a word" with Juan and the twins.

Chapter Four

It was a dry autumn, golden with mist and dust. The leaves on the trees in the square looked tired with summer but hung on. My sun-tan stayed too, without peeling or going dirty. Trog changed jobs and went to live in Norwich, which Mum minded more than she wanted us to see. Marco occasionally appeared from Cambridge looking incredibly spruce because he was seeing TV people about getting his Andes film shown. He had rows with Dad because he wanted to take up a job he'd been offered with a fly-by-night film company instead of taking his degree. They weren't loud rows—we don't do that—but they made the house feel less comfortable. Adam was slogging away for his Oxbridge exams, in November. I used to drop around and listen to his records while he read or wrote, but we practically never went out to pubs or films or saw any of our usual friends. It was a bit like being married, I suppose.

Several times, because of the weather, Mum and Dad and I almost made a dash down to the cottage for the weekend, but the journey and the opening-up and then the shutting-up and the journey back always seemed just a bit too much, though by Sunday evening we'd all three be wishing we'd done it. It felt as though it was going to be autumn for ever.

Only the opera seemed to bring the winter nearer. As usual we had a main rehearsal every Monday, 4.45 to 6.45 in theory but actually 5.05 to 7.15 at least. It was like a very slow heart-beat, a pulse only once a week, followed by the sick feeling of another whole rehearsal gone, and everything still such a mess,

and so much to do before December and the actual performances. We would spend the first hour in the church, with the
children learning and practising the bits which the whole cast
sang, and then we'd split up into groups to do the separate
numbers in the two vestries and some of the houses round the
square, leaving the church free for Prue to rehearse the dances.
Bill swore that he'd deliberately written the opera so that it
could be taken apart, rehearsed piecemeal and reassembled at the
last minute, but most of the time it just seemed an incredible
muddle.

In the end I decided there was no point in having any kind of
"word" with the twins. It wasn't that I funked it—I just knew it
wouldn't work. Anything I asked them to do they'd do the
opposite. If I told them we'd turf them out they wouldn't
mind—it'd just add to their idea of themselves as unstoppable
little toughies, and screw up their Mum's pottery classes as a
bonus. The only hope was to get Juan to see that if he didn't
react to their needling they'd lay off. I thought I might manage
that—he looked a pretty bright kid—but I guessed it wouldn't
be any use talking to him with anyone else around—he'd be too
determined to show them he wasn't taking orders from a
woman. So I rang up the Embassy and spoke to Senora
O'Grady.

"He is not being a good boy?" she said.

"Well, it's not really his fault. He gets into fights."

She laughed. "You wish me to tell my son not to have fights
with other boys? I do not think it is possible."

"I suppose not. I just thought . . . if I could talk to him alone
for a bit."

"Any time you wish. You will come here?"

"That'd be making too much of a thing of it. I thought, if I
just happened to be passing the Embassy next time he's on his
way to a rehearsal, the car might stop and give me a lift. Ferdy
could pretend to recognise me."

She laughed again. I'd only seen her once, and thought she
looked simply terrifying, beautiful, grand and icy, but her laugh
was amazingly warm and friendly.

"He is young to begin being deceived by women," she said.
"Very good, I will give the instructions."

We settled the exact time and rang off.

That part of the conspiracy worked a dream. The embassy Rolls
slid up the driveway just as I was passing. Ferdy, sitting in front
beside the chauffeur, waved. The car stopped. I opened the back
door and hopped in. Juan looked distinctly pleased to see me.

"That's a bit of luck," I said. "I was going to be late at the
church. I say, what a super bus."

Juan bounced forward on his seat and rapped on the window.

"Bullet-proof," he said. "Pow! Pow!"

"Is it really? Why on earth? You don't think . . . ? In
England . . . ?"

He flung himself back, looking at me out of the corner of his
eyes, scorning my ignorance and innocence. But almost at once
he bounced up again, flipped a lid in the arm-rest beside him and
pressed one of a row of buttons. In front of me, under the glass
screen which divided the rear compartment from the front seats,
a section of quilted black leather swung down and then forward,
becoming a neat little table. In the rack behind were glasses and
decanters.

"Drink?" said Juan.

"No thanks. Listen, I'm glad to see you because . . ."

He pressed more buttons. The table disappeared and a television screen popped out on the other side of the partition.

"You like Star Trek?" he said.

"Yuck," I said. "Listen. Do you want the opera to work?"

"Sure."

"Well it's not going to if you and the twins keep fighting in
rehearsals."

Quite deliberately he turned away and did something with his control panel. The sound came on, and then the picture. It was the advertisements—a pretty little girl in a frilly frock asking for fish fingers for her birthday party, and then a lot of other kids in grown-up clothes pretending to be shoppers at some Oxford Street store, and then . . . honestly, I don't know where they get all those plastic children from, to sell things with. I was making up my mind whether to lean across and try and switch the thing off when Juan did it himself.

"They make me fight," he said. "If they make me, I've got to."

"I don't see it," I said. "I mean, they're only needling you because they know you'll blow up. By getting into scraps with them you're doing what they want."

"I've got to," he said again.

"Why? To show you're tougher than they are? What's the point?"

"The point is honour," he said.

I stared, but luckily he wasn't looking at me, or he'd have guessed I was thinking how absurd it was for a kid his age to talk like that. I wasn't, actually. I was amazed all right, but only by being brought up suddenly against his sheer differentness from the rest of the children. It was more than just foreignness. It was a completely different way of seeing the world. I realised there was no point in trying to argue him out of it—telling him for instance that it'd be much more grown-up if he treated the twins' needling as too childish to pay any attention to. In any case there wasn't much time. The Rolls was already waiting for a moment to nose into the commuter-jam at the bottom of Holland Park Avenue, and once it had found a slot we'd be at the church in another couple of minutes.

"OK," I said. "You realise that if there are many more fights you'll all three get turfed out, war or no war."

"I've got to," he muttered.

His face was set. He glared at me. All at once I guessed that he really longed to be in the opera, that somehow it meant almost as much to him as it had to me when I was that age, but that even so he'd rather get chucked out than give one inch on a point of honour. The Rolls whimpered forward under the plane trees.

"All right," I said. "I'll do what I can. Just don't you start anything. And listen, I may have to ask Ferdy to help me. If I do, he's going to have to treat you exactly the same as all the others, and you're going to have to let yourself be treated like that. Understand? That's a point of honour too."

He nodded, very serious, then relaxed and grinned at me. When the Rolls stopped at the church I was reaching for the door handle but he stopped me. We waited while Ferdy got out and looked carefully up and down the road before opening the door for us. As we went into the church I was thinking about Juan, and what it must be like to be bred and brought up to ideas like he had, and an assumption of danger like he had too.

Mercifully one of the twins was away sick for that rehearsal. Even so I only just managed to keep the pot from boiling over by sitting behind the ravens and breathing down their necks all the way through. I knew I'd never manage it if both the twins were there, so as soon as it was over I collared Mr Slim and told him what I wanted him to say to Ferdy. In fact Ferdy had already pushed off with Juan, but Mr Slim promised he'd get onto him during the week. I made a mental note to remind him at least twice.

I met Toby on the steps of Mrs Banks's just before the third rehearsal. I'd gone round to collect the key to open the church. It was raining—the first rain for weeks—and Toby came prancing up the steps under a huge yellow and green golf brolly.

"Doll, darling," he warbled. "The very lass! Hooray! Come in under here. There's something I want to ask you."

I felt suspicious. When Toby does his jolly-hockey-sticks turn it usually means that he's trying to get you to do something you won't fancy.

"Dear Dave Slim," he said. "You know what he's like, *so* willing and eager, but musically . . . ah, well."

"We wouldn't get anywhere without him," I said.

"Of *course* not. But listen—you know that colossally handsome Valentino chappie who's been coming to rehearsals?"

"Ferdy? Yes."

"Well now. The raven song-and-dance act—it's got a guitar backing."

"I thought it was pizzicato strings."

"Bill's changed his mind. He met this guitarist and rescored the whole bloody thing. But the chap's a professional and can't make it to rehearsals."

"Do you want me to see if I . . . ?"

"No, no, sweetie—not that I'm deriding your prowess on the keys. But it's going to sound so different on the piano, you see. It'll throw those kids if they have to make the change at the last moment. I want them to rehearse to guitar, if poss. But now Dave Slim's been talking to your dishy friend . . ."

"I asked him to try and get Ferdy to control the ravens."

"So it's all your fault! Even if you didn't ask him to tell your friend to bring his guitar to the rehearsals and accompany the ravens."

"No!"

"Yes, sweetie."

"But is he any good?"

"That's just the point—no one knows, and *you're* going to have to find out."

"Me? But . . ."

"Yes, you. And don't tell me you couldn't have foreseen that Dave and your friend would somehow get onto the subject of guitars. You know perfectly well that it's Dave's greatest pleasure in life to pick some oddment up in the street and work it into the opera."

"But I can't . . ."

"Don't worry, poppet. Bill will be there, but . . . Honestly, I don't want the ravens croaking cha-cha-chas, and Bill's perfectly capable of deciding that's what he wants or rewriting it again in rumba rhythm. I shan't get any sense out of Bill, whether your friend can play or not. Composers are rotten judges, you know, fretting over trifles nobody's going to hear and not noticing stuff that really matters. I doubt if he's even grasped that the raven song is the most original number in the whole shoot. Don't look so appalled, dovie—if you're in the mafia you've got to take things on, you know. And if Bill's there somebody else simply must be. Remember what happened with poor old Thornie. So just look after it for me, ducks. Lovely. Hooray!"

I had a vile first half of rehearsal, worrying. I kept wishing Toby hadn't mentioned Dame Doris Thorne—he calls her Thornie. She's a colossally grand singing-teacher—she's supposed to be retired now but even the Covent Garden stars who used to be her pupils still plug out to Chiswick for a work-out with her when they're in London. Because she's a friend of Toby's she used to come to the opera always, and usually to a couple of rehearsals to teach some of the soloists how to get a bit more volume without beginning to bawl, until Bill's first year when he told her to her face she was telling them to make the wrong sort of noise, and even Toby couldn't smooth things over and she never came again. Of course Bill didn't think he was being rude—he was just stating a fact and he couldn't see why Dame Doris should have minded any more than Bill would have minded if somebody had told him he wasn't cut out for tight-rope walking.

The first half of that rehearsal went badly enough anyway, with the children on their most unspeakable behaviour, so that Toby actually lost his temper instead of just pretending to, and Mum tensed up and there were muddles about which bar they were starting on and so on . . . and I sat at the back thinking of Ferdy clumsily strumming cha-cha-chas and Bill saying something unforgivable and Ferdy drawing his famous gun . . . no, not really, but I do hate rows and I didn't want Ferdy's feelings hurt. He was very sweet and simple when you got to know him, and he'd certainly taken control of the ravens in a way no one else could have done.

But it was all right. At last Toby blew his whistle and there was the usual clamour and clatter as the children jostled their way out to the rehearsal houses while two idiot mums tried to exchange gossip in the doorway and didn't think of moving aside. I found Bill in the sacristy, of all places. He'd discovered where Onward hides the key and was reading the letters on Onward's desk. He didn't seem at all ashamed. I took him to the back vestry.

The ravens were already there, sitting in a row on the brown linoleum, legs crossed, silent. Ferdy, as usual, shook hands with Bill, then turned to the children. His face changed slightly.

"I say Tim this end and Tom that end," he said softly. "Why you not do what I say you?"

The twins' eyes widened.

He flickered an eyelid at me.

"You've had a look at the score?" said Bill. "Think you can manage?"

"Very difficult," said Ferdy. "The beat very difficult."

"Oh, I don't know," said Bill. "Takes a bit of getting used to, I suppose, but . . . Look."

He spread out the score on the top of the terrible upright piano—we never use it if we can help—and started tapping and clucking and humming and wagging his head about. Ferdy craned beside him. The children watched, absolutely quiet. I was puzzled by the look on their faces—anxious, almost pleading—until I realised they were worried Ferdy wasn't going to be able to play the music. Worried not for their sake, or the opera or the wasted evening, but for him. It was extraordinary. Except for Juan they hardly knew him. He bossed them around, made them sit quiet on the hard floor, and yet they adored him. They were Ferdy fans, besotted as any screaming kids scrambling for a sight of their pop idol. Anything Ferdy did he had to do better than anyone else. Their faces fell when he shook his head and pursed his lips.

"Maybe I practise a little," he said. "You tell to the kids your historia, uh?"

"Right you are," said Bill. "Once you've got that eleven-sixteen beat into your head you'll find the rest of it's quite straightforward, apart from the odd cross-rhythm."

"Sure," said Ferdy, and took the score over into the far corner where he had leaned his guitar against the vestment wardrobe. He plucked away softly, two or three notes at a time, while Bill explained to the children about Elijah running off to the desert to escape from Jezebel's swordsmen.

"You've got to imagine it," he said. "He's crawled out among these burning hills, dying of thirst, and he's found one little trickle of water seeping between two rocks. He's saved—but soon he realises he's trapped, too. He's so weak that he can't go back the way he's come. If he leaves the water he'll die of thirst, and if he stays where he is he'll die of hunger. Then, down, down out of nowhere, float these great black birds, croaking like demons. Let's hear you croak. Oh, come off it, that's not ravens, that's frogs or something. That's more like it. But you're not supposed to be English rooks, you're great Syrian ravens, and you make a croak that sort of trails off. Aargha-ay. No, harsher, slower . . . Someone's got it! You!"

He pointed. Queenie Windsor, solemn and smug, gathered herself into a slow croak. The others copied her. The boys started competing to see who could make the most racket. Bill began to flap his hands about to stop them, but it was no use till Ferdy strolled over and raised a finger. They fell silent and he went back to his guitar. I noticed that he was stringing more notes together now.

"Right," said Bill. "So you've got old Elijah out in the desert watching these ugly great birds. His first thought is they're waiting for him to die so they can peck out his eyes. Then he thinks that if he could only catch one or two he'd have something to eat, but they're too clever for him. Prue will fix what you do, but you've got to know the music first. Now imagine, all this time the birds are circling around, croaking and cawing . . . oh for God's sake shut up! That's better. But gradually, gradually—and this is what you've got to get bang right—the sound of the croaking changes, until it becomes a word, a name, *the* name . . . Know what I'm talking about? Oh, come on, how thick can you get? Whose side are you on in this opera? Not Baal's, are you? Right, now croak—you. And now say the name in the same kind of voice. Got it? OK . . . Oh, shut up! That's just what we don't want. Obvious, boring. The name's got to grow out of the cawing softly, slowly, so that no one notices what's happening until it's *there*, and *then* they realise it's been there all along only they were too deaf to hear. Because *that's* what Elijah finds. He should have known from the start they were Yahweh's birds, only he was too busy worrying about whether they were going to peck his eyes out or thinking about how to trap and eat them, right?

"That's why I've written every croak and caw into your music, so that you do it bang on time and the whole thing isn't a mess—though it'll sound like one to people who don't know what's going to happen. You're going to have to know every bar of the music, even when it's not your turn to caw. I'd better explain about the backing. It begins as a bird-dance, jerky and flapping . . . think you can do us the first eight bars, Mr . . . er . . . er . . . ?"

"Ferdy," said Ferdy. "Sure. I try."

He bent himself over the strings. I noticed how small and neat his hands were. When he began to play it was difficult to know whether the jerkiness was his fault or what Bill wanted.

"It'll have to go quite a bit faster," said Bill.

"I practise at home."

"OK. Now, you kids, you wouldn't guess that was going to turn into the Yahweh music, would you, but it does, without anybody noticing. Those eight bars change a little every time they come round until all at once you're cawing the name of Yahweh and the band's belting out the Yahweh music and Elijah's singing his solo about Yahweh and the whole church is ringing with the glory of the God of Israel. If you get it right it'll be terrific, uh?"

Typically Bill had begun by remembering he was talking to children but by now he was gabbling about three times the speed of light, almost frothing at the mouth with the excitement of his own ideas. It sounded a very Bill sort of notion. He loves things changing into other things—not just the words and music, either. Mr Slim's top headache was turning out to be the tower Bill wanted, so that Elijah had somewhere to fly up to in his fiery chariot and Jezebel had somewhere to be thrown down from so that the dogs could eat her. She had to fall in slow motion, too, screaming as she went. Screaming in tune. Dear old Bill.

Something like a battering ram slammed into the vestry door. There's a type of boy who simply cannot imagine that door-handles are for anything except decoration, and we seem always to have half a dozen of them in the opera, so I wasn't surprised. But I was aware of a quick, quiet movement in Ferdy's corner as I went to open the door. Peter Banks stood there, panting. He's twelve. He refuses to have a part in the opera, but loves running messages, and manages to make the most minor problem sound like the last straw.

"Bill?" he gasped. "Mum says can you come over? They're having a terrific row about the Naboth's Vineyard song. It's the repeats."

"Oh Lord, I knew there was something . . . I haven't made up my mind. OK, Pete—you can manage now here, Doll?"

"If Ferdy . . ."

I turned to look for him. He was standing by the corner of the big vestment wardrobe. He saw me watching him and winked, but I was aware of an oddness, as if he was just now relaxing from some kind of sudden effort. His hand was stroking down the front of his jacket, straightening it, but again that didn't look quite natural. I couldn't be sure, but I felt that out of the corner of my eye I'd seen him actually coming out from beyond the wardrobe, and at the same time putting something back into the inside breast pocket of his jacket. Suddenly I remembered what he was—a bodyguard. I remembered the way Peter had barged into the door, and what that might have sounded like to somebody who wasn't used to it. And perhaps Juan hadn't been just boasting when he told me that Ferdy carried a gun.

Bill gawked away. We settled down to numbering the ravens so that they could learn which one had to croak when. We even got them to rehearse the first twenty bars before it was time to pack in.

I reached the mafia session after Toby had left.

"He wanted you to ring him in the morning," said Mum. "I told him you'd be at school before he was out of bed, so he's ringing me about eleven."

"Tell him Ferdy's OK," I said. "Quite good, honestly. Pretty slow, still, though."

"No harm while they're learning," said Mum. "Provided he can speed up in a week or two."

"He's taken the score home to practise," I said. "I bet you he'll be spot on next week. Have you seen it? Eleven-sixteen, honestly, and Bill hardly sticks even to that for more than three bars at a time. A few cross-rhythms, my foot!"

"Don't tell me this is one of those scenes where everybody's going to have to watch Toby the whole time," said Mrs Dunnitt.

(It was just the three of us by the fire. The others were up by the piano, sorting out some snag to do with the insurance.)

"Not half," I said. "Every blessed step and croak."

Mrs Dunnitt blew a scornful jet of smoke down her tweed jacket.

"Absurd," she said. "I'm asked to provide them with

enormous beaks and great flapping wings. They're hardly going to be able to see *anything*, on top of which they'll have their backs to Toby half the time."

"They'll just have to be drilled and drilled until they can do it blindfold," said Mum.

"I don't see anybody drilling that particular set of brats," said Mrs Dunnitt.

"Oh, Ferdy can," I said. "He's got them eating out of his hand. If they need drilling, he'll drill them."

"That's an unfortunate turn of phrase," snapped Mrs Dunnitt.

It took me a moment to understand why I'd upset her.

"But he isn't like that, really he isn't," I told her. "He's rather sweet, and the children adore him, and he's getting very wrapped up in the opera too. He keeps saying sensible things about the music, and I bet he practises that part all week even though he's only doing it for the rehearsals. You know, *you'd* have had to practise quite a bit, Mum."

"I've never cared much for pizzicato at the best of times," said Mum.

Mrs Dunnitt lit another cigarette, drew on it and sat staring at the carpet.

"At least having this thug involved in things has made me think," she said. "I've been lying awake in the small hours and wondering. You know, so far I've always done the opera as if it had no connection with anything else in the world. It was sheer self-indulgence, a way of going back to my own childhood, and the fun of getting the old costumes out of the big padded chest and dressing up. I closed my eyes to the fact that the children I was dressing up now were going to grow into what I believe to be the enemies of society, and that I was helping in the process, reinforcing their picture of their life as being right and normal. It all seemed too vague to make much fuss about—after all, most of the people I work with for the things I regard as important have some sort of indulgence—they drink fine wines or collect tobacco-tins or . . ."

"But of course," said Mum. "You have to be a saint not to have some kind of outlet, and saints make everyone else's life hell. I'm sure you've been a better Party member—if that's what you are—by letting yourself go once a year."

"So I've told myself in the past," said Mrs Dunnitt. "But now . . ."

She sighed again and dragged heavily at her cigarette. I was appalled. It was impossible to think of going on without her. Well, I suppose not—some of the mums are quite clever with masks or costumes, but I couldn't think of anyone else who'd be able to keep everything under control so that it all seems to belong. It's not just a question of every child having something that fits and looks pretty—it's the way Mrs Dunnitt's costumes seem to help each other so that we don't have to build a lot of scenery and stuff to make the audience feel they're looking at a real, rich, magic world.

Without noticing what I was doing I said again, "But he isn't like that. Really he isn't."

Mrs Dunnitt was sitting on the big stool by the fireside, so that she had had to twist her head awkwardly to look at me. Now she turned herself right round so that she could stare up into my eyes. She's so brisk and leathery-tough that usually you don't think of her as being much older than Mum and the others, but suddenly she looked almost as old as the Grannies.

"My dear Doll," she said, "you can't tell. How easy it would be if you could. If only those who like lovely music were therefore lovely people. If only those who are good with children were therefore good in every other way. I tell you, there are professional torturers in the world who go home from their ghastly work like a man going home from his office, and they kiss their wives and read a bedtime story to their children and after supper they put on a record of the Mozart Requiem and listen to it with real appreciation. Art is no salvation. Art is no excuse."

Her voice was a kind of tearing whisper. She leaned forward

on her stool and watched me with dry, pale, unblinking eyes, appalled and sad. Not sad for herself, but sad for me and all the world.

"I can't believe that," said Mum. "I'm quite sure we'd all be worse off without it. It's everything that makes life worth living."

Mrs Dunnitt just shook her head and breathed slow smoke, watching me still.

"All right," I said. "Let's say you can't tell. But it works the other way too, doesn't it? Ferdy might be a good guy. I mean, he might have got himself this job because he doesn't want to live in Matteo, if it's the way you say it is."

"It makes no difference," said Mrs Dunnitt. "He is involved, even if he has done nothing with his own hands."

"I'm going to ask him," I said.

"Do that," she said. "Only don't tell me the answer. Do it for your own sake . . . don't worry, Elsie—I'm not going to pull out on you. I'll see the darned thing through. Let's think about these ravens. If I tell the Maclean woman to make top-of-the-head masks after all, and we persuade Prue to manage the dance so that the brats are moving in Toby's direction when it's their turn to come in . . ."

I asked Ferdy next Monday, before the rehearsal. Some of the Jezebel handmaids had slid over from the Baal pews and were clustered round him as if they were supposed to be there, and Veronica Drew was actually chatting him up. She was wearing eye make-up thick as mud pies too. She's thirteen. I shooed them back to their places and sat down next to Ferdy. He winked at me. He hadn't tried his tiger trick since that first time —I expect he'd seen in my face I didn't like it, but with a lot of men that would only have made them still more macho. Just another way in which Mrs Dunnitt didn't understand what kind of person Ferdy was.

"I want to ask you something," I said.

"Sure."

"Don't be angry. It's to settle an argument. Are you a member of the PDS?"

He was puzzled, though I'd found he could pick up most of what you said to him and could smatter along happily in English once he was sure you weren't going to laugh at him. Perhaps he just didn't understand my pronunciation of the letters, for a moment. Then his frown changed. He didn't seem angry, but he seemed to be watching me carefully, and from much further away, though we hadn't moved.

"Why you ask?" he said.

I began to stammer and blush. I suppose I could have come along with a nice, smooth, harmless reason for wanting to know, but I expect my stammering helped, really. A smooth reason would have made him still more suspicious. He shook his head sadly, as if I'd spilt a jug of milk and he was going to do his best to clear up the mess and not blame me for my clumsiness.

"Listen," he said. "I am telling you yes . . . *If* I am telling you yes . . . you tell to . . ."

He shrugged his shoulders.

"I wouldn't tell anyone, honestly," I said.

"This argument . . .? But listen, you are saying to someone 'Ferdy is in PDS', uh? I go home, to Matteo. I sit in the cafe, read the football. Auto come . . . plenty autos at cafe. This one stop, quick. I look from my paper, see auto, see gun . . . Too late! Tat-tat-tat-tat! Brrahrrm, and car gone. Ferdy gone too, gone for always."

He wasn't making it up. He gave me an angry little smile.

"You people," he said. "All places must be same with England. Same police, same politic, same food, same families . . ."

He paused, watching me. I looked away and saw Mum standing by the piano. She was talking to Jake Laver, obviously about his part—Jake takes his music dead seriously—craning forward, eager, happy . . .

"I got no family ," said Ferdy. "Is lucky for me, now. I tell you. My father is police, normal police. His work is kids taking autos, men fighting at bodega, women using knife on other woman who take their man, bank-bandits, all that. Normal, never politic. In that time Matteo got civil government, terrorismo only commence a little, along by mountains. Then government make plan to estabilise places of terrorismo—they give two times pension to servants of government when they go to live in these places. Understand? My father take pension, buy small estancia under mountains—in his heart he is always farmer, not police—vines, tomatoes, maize, melons. And so beautiful to live there, good family, mother, father, two aunts, Ferdy, Ferdy's sister. Father careful man, say to nobody once he was police. Two years, and I go to college in San Matteo, where father was in police. I take photograph—the estancia, my family, my sister. I say prayers each night to God to be guarding them. Each week I write letters, my mother write to me, long letters. One week, no letter. Two weeks, no letter. Is no telephone in our estancia, so I must telephone to post office in our small town. They are most surprised I do not know. They tell me two Sundays before the terroristos come with fire-bombs when all my family is asleep, and all are dead, burnt while they sleep. My sister, she is same age with you, Miss Doll."

"That's dreadful!" I whispered. "How could they?"

"Easy. It is the rationale of terrorismo. They do not wish the estabilisation to operate. They choose my family for the exemplum, so no more servants of the government are coming. They announce to the newspapers this is their rationale. And I have no family."

I was still trying to think of something to say when Mum banged her chord and Toby blew his whistle and the yelling stopped.

"What a relief," said Toby. "Lovely, lovely silence, to be followed by lovely, lovely singing. New song. This is your first really big number. Some of it Ahab is singing solo, some of it you're joining him, and some of it you're drowning him out with the Yahweh shout and the Baal shout. You know those, so we'll kick off teaching you your part of the Ahab music. Page two, first chorus—He's the king in the middle—got it? Right, it goes like this—and please, *please* don't join in. Elsie . . .

> He's the king in the middle,
>   He's the king in a muddle,
> In a muddle in the middle,
>   In the middle in a muddle—
>   What'll he do?
>   What'll he do?
>   What'll he do?"

Chapter Five

Monday . . . and another Monday . . . and another Monday . . .

Appallingly soon it was half-term. In theory the rehearsals are for the music up till half-term and Toby's in charge. Then everybody takes a week off, and then the rest of the rehearsals are for Prue to get the movements right because the children are supposed to know the music by now.

I don't remember one year when it really worked. There's always been bits of music still to learn at half-term, and in any case the children forget half of what they did know as soon as they're expected to do anything except sit in their pews and sing. They don't forget it completely, they just slop back into all the bad habits Toby's been fighting to get them out of. It's only when you've worked with somebody like Toby you find how the difference between an exciting sound and a boring one can be as little as a tenth of a second at the point at which one note comes in a bar. With Bill's music everything seems to be not quite on the beat, and of course the children keep putting it bang on, and Toby has to butt into Prue's rehearsal time and get it right again before the wrongness becomes a habit.

So we get more and more behindhand, and the mafia start fitting in extra rehearsals which weren't in the original schedule, which everybody hates—parents because it means another evening hanging around to ferry kids home—it's dark by now, of course, with summer-time officially ending and all the clocks going back—and worrying about the kids getting their home-work done and their supper eaten before bedtime, and so on.

The children don't like it either, the big ones partly because of the homework business and the way it cuts into their social lives, the smalls because inevitably there's some TV series they're hooked on on the extra day that's been chosen. It's unpopular with Onward, too, because it means asking whoever else was supposed to be using the church that evening—the Brownies or the meditators or the Morris Dancers—to change their times; and for the mafia's own families it means yet another messed-up evening.

You seem to be rehearsing all the time. Even the Mondays somehow come closer together, because there's so much to fit in. The change from summer-time makes it worse—when the children were coming in in T-shirts and it was still daylight so they could get home by themselves there was a feeling of time to spare and December and the actual performances still ages off. But after half-term it's darkish even before the rehearsals start and the children come in with their anoraks glinting with rain— this year November turned specially vile, with sheets of wet followed by bitter cold—and by the end there are twenty mums and a few dads sitting in the back pews and grabbing your sleeve and asking when it's going to *finish*, for heaven's sake, and you don't know either . . . Then you begin to feel the real pressure.

A bit after half-term Dad had a session with me about my own homework. He was ultra-reasonable, considering he passion-ately wants me to get accepted for his old college at Oxford—a bit ironic, as he can't really get used to the idea of their letting women in at all. Trog and Marco went to Cambridge so I'll have to do, for all the shame of having a *daughter* in those hallowed halls. I don't mind bitterly about it either way, myself, which is lucky as those posh old colleges take about one girl in twenty who try. My view is that if I'm going to bother at all I might as well go all out, so it won't be my fault if I don't make it. I don't expect to sail in on brains alone. My brains aren't that special. Last term's report had a note from the Surmistress saying I was clearly an ant, not a grasshopper. Too true to be funny.

Anyway, Dad rabbited on about me doing too much for the opera, and helping Mr Slim paint his scenery and Mrs Dunnitt sew her costumes and getting generally exploited by the mafia, so that I didn't have time for my schoolwork. He'd spotted I'd been up till half-past two the night before, and I had to let on I'd been doing notes for the Baal priests about an extra rehearsal, but I swore I'd still been bright as a lark all day. (I bet even larks have off days, when they don't feel like going up more than a few yards, tweeting around a bit and sliding off home.) In the end I got him off the subject by asking if he was going to help with the scaffolding this year.

"Try and keep me out," he said.

"It's going to be the biggest ever."

"Goody, goody."

Putting up the scaffolding is our great comic turn. A dozen dads gather at the church late one evening, clutching spanners and bottles of wine. The poles and clamps have been delivered by the hirers that day, and the dads immediately fall on them, like small boys with a giant Meccano set, and start waving them about and fixing bits together. They're always far too eager to get on with the fun to bother working out the right way of going about things, so quite soon there's a total muddle, with dads at the tops of ladders dropping clamps onto dads who are doing something different at ground level, while two or three master minds stand around shouting contradictory instructions until they get a tottery structure up and then they all swarm onto it like apes on a climbing-frame, trying to make it less tottery, except that then someone goes and loosens a vital clamp and the whole contraption sways and they all swarm down white and shaking and have another swig of wine . . . Onward used to fuss terribly about them knocking chips off his church until they persuaded him to come and help and now he turns up with a much bigger spanner than anyone else's and gouges great strips of plaster out with pole-ends and laughs his super-jolly laugh and says, "Just a scratch, my dear fellow, just a scratch. Nothing like making the old place look lived in, eh?"

The scaffolding tends to get bigger each year. It started because the dais is too low to make a proper stage, and then they found that if you've got a hundred children in the cast it's much more effective if you can spread them out upwards rather than having them massed all at one level so that the audience only see the front row and a lot of head-dresses behind. This year, what with Mount Carmel and Jezebel's tower and the heaven for the fiery chariot to go up into and the fire of Yahweh to come down from, Mr Slim—I'd seen his model—was going to block the chancel arch off completely. I made a mental note to make Dad wear a hard hat.

I hope you haven't got the impression the opera would have ground to a halt without me. Of course they'd have got on almost as well, give or take a few muddles and things like cleaning up the sweet-wrappers after rehearsals. And there were masses of things I had nothing to do with. The lights, for instance. Mr Tolland always does them, which is why Hattie has to have a part, painful though her voice is. He's a heavy, pale, stupid-sounding man who works for Thames TV, but every year he does amazing things with the lights. "Fire. From. Heaven," he says, speaking slowly like a policeman writing down your name with a blunt pencil, but you know that bang on cue, as Elijah flings up his arm at the end of his prayer to Yahweh, somehow the lightning will spear down and the sacrifice will burst into flames and the audience will thrill with amazement, all because Mr Tolland has slid a few controls up or down and pressed a couple of switches. He gets his own scaffolding up for his lights, too. He and his brother do it between them at three o'clock one morning in the run-up week, with no fuss whatever.

I didn't have anything to do with the money or the tickets or the seating or the insurance or the scaffold-hire or even the orchestra. Dad was a bit mean to bring up the painting for Mr Slim—it had only been one Saturday afternoon when Adam was in a bitchy mood so I left him to it and found Mr Slim making collapsible Baals in his workshop. He's a wizard at making things work and knocking up ingenious answers to Prue's problems from bits of old timber he collects from building sites, but he draws and paints like a small child. He'd made his Baals as human-headed bulls—rough papier mache—and I had a go at the faces.

That was all the painting I did, and the sewing wasn't much more. It was the Saturday after. Mum was practising, and all of a sudden I was sick of the sound. Sometimes I feel as though I've had the voice of the Testori in my ears every instant of my life since I was born, rather the way people who live by the sea have the smell and feel and sound of it with them all the time until it's so deep in their bones that somehow they become different from other people. Unmusical friends who hear the Testori for the first time are often a bit disappointed. It isn't one of your super-mellow, oh-what-a-lovely-tone instruments, though of course Mum can get that sort of noise out of it if she wants to. But its natural tone sounds rough, almost gritty—"masculine" they call it. (Like being kissed by a bloke who hasn't shaved for a couple of days, do you think they mean?) Really it's a big, rich, thrilling sound, and I love it, but that morning Mum was working away at something ultra-modern and showy, with a lot of rapid heel-of-the-bow stuff right at the top of the register, the same dozen bars over and over and over, nag, nag, nag. I was supposed to be writing an essay on Cromwell and the Puritans, which surprisingly enough I found quite interesting— a bit like old Ahab's problems with Elijah in some ways—but Mum's scrapings were coming up through two floors of the house and once I'd started noticing them they got more and more on my nerves until I simply couldn't think about anything else. I stopped writing in the middle of the sentence and almost ran out of the house. It was only when I was standing on the pavement that I realised I hadn't anywhere I particularly wanted to go. I chose Mrs Dunnitt almost at random.

The church stands in the middle of a square, all built over a hundred years ago. Apparently the first builder had pretty grand ideas about who was going to buy his houses, so three and a half sides of the square are really handsome, with extra-tall rooms and round-topped windows on the ground floor and so on. Our own house, and the Banks' and most of our other friends' are like that, and we often find TV crews out in the square making commercials which want a posh and tasteful background— probably for some ghastly product which none of us would be seen dead with. Only that first builder got his sums wrong and couldn't find enough nobby people to buy his grand houses and went bankrupt, so the last half-side of the square was finished off by a builder who squeezed an extra floor into every house and wasn't bothered by trimmings like round-topped windows. They're perfectly good houses—not slums—but you don't get TV crews making commercials on their doorsteps. Most of them are split up into flats, and though plenty of children live there practically none of them are the sort who join the opera. Mrs Dunnitt is the exception. She lives in the ground-floor flat of 58.

I'd often been there, to have costumes fitted, but I can't ever really have looked at Mrs Dunnitt's room—I suppose I'd always been too wrapped up in what *I* was going to look like to worry about the appearance of anything else. In my mind's eye there was just a long, light room, windows at opposite ends, stained boards and lots of rugs, all piled with mounds of gaudy cloth and devil-masks on stands and racks of robes on wire hangers. This time I saw that for the rest of the year it might be rather a bleak and dreary place. There was shelf after shelf of books, lots of them with the sort of yellow wrappers you used to get on detective stories. No real pictures, but dozens of posters. Actually I'd vaguely remembered these but I'd always thought of them as theatre posters, but now I saw that they said things

like SUPPORT THE MINERS' STRUGGLE and REMEM-
BER SACCO, REMEMBER VANZETTI and SECOND
FRONT NOW and FREE NELSON MANDELA. Some of
them were very yellow and old.

Just to have an excuse for visiting her I'd asked Mrs Dunnitt
whether she wanted any help with the sewing. Now she slid a
green gauzy dress out of one of the racks and waved it at me.

"Idiot woman," she snapped.

"Me?"

"Of course not. The Drew female. Look."

She draped the costume in front of her. The gauze settled in
swirls. There were silver trimmings across the bust. I thought it
was immensely pretty.

"I wouldn't mind wearing that for a party," I said.

"Exactly. I gave her the stuff. I showed her the drawing, I
explained what I wanted, and she came back with *this*. Look how
she's done it—everything French-seamed and tucked and rucked
and goodness knows what. Honestly, idiot though she clearly is,
I'd have thought she'd have known better. She's supposed to be
some kind of actress, isn't she?"

"Oh, I don't expect she sewed it herself. I think the Drews have
got a nanny, and now that Katie . . ."

"That explains it. Nursery-work, of course. Why didn't I think
of that? Well, it'll take three times as long to unpick as if she'd
done it the way I told her. Will you do that for me? Here's my
seam-ripper. Get rid of all this gathering for a start."

I took the ripper and the costume and found a stool. Mrs
Dunnitt sat down at her ancient Singer—it ought to be in a
museum—and banged away at the treadle. I soon found out what
she meant about the costume.

"I wish I could sew like this," I said when I'd unpicked a couple
of inches.

"You wouldn't be any good to me if you could, my dear."

"I don't . . ."

"Most people don't. Tacked, I tell them, tacked. But can they bring themselves to do it? They can't understand that if you sew like a nursery-maid you'll get an effect like a child's tea-party-frock. Theatre is all about gesture. It's the gesture that carries the meaning. If you try to make something more *than* a gesture you'll finish up making it less *of* a gesture. You don't want real dresses on a stage any more than you want real murders."

She banged away at her treadle. I could hear the machine gobbling through the cloth in clumsy coarse stitches. She was sewing a yard while I unpicked an inch. After a bit I looked up and my eye was caught by a poster in German—it still looked like a poster for a play. I wondered whether it was as old as before the war—it looked it—some protest against the Nazis—and only this summer she'd been on her vigil outside the Mattean Embassy . . . Did it ever end . . . ?

Mrs Dunnitt stopped pedalling.

"Did you really come to help?" she said.

I snatched up the costume.

"I'm sorry," I said. "I was thinking what a lot of those . . ."

She laughed. I think it was the first time I'd heard her do that. Her laugh wasn't like her voice, much more relaxed and cheerful.

"All theatre, too," she said. "All gestures. That doesn't mean they weren't important. Often a gesture is the only action you can take, you know. That's how I came to be interested in costumes . . . oh, long ago, before Hitler, even. I married my husband when I was just out of school and he took me to Berlin. He was going through a stage when he thought he might become a theatrical director and he wanted to meet Brecht. Nothing came of it, except that I found myself earning a little money sewing costumes in Reinhardt's theatre, and watching rehearsals and learning about gesture . . ."

Her dry voice sounded amused, not sad. She hauled her work out of the machine, flapped it straight and began to pin a fresh seam. I picked away at the neat little gatherings and thought about what she'd told me.

"I suppose one of the problems with gestures is that it's harder to tell when you're wrong," I said.

"What do you mean?"

"Well, if you do something which isn't a gesture . . . er . . ."

"Take direct action?"

"Yes. If you do that you can tell whether it's working or not. If it isn't, you stop. But gestures . . ."

"Are you thinking of anything in particular?"

I hadn't been—or perhaps I had, subconsciously, starting with imagining her vigilling away outside the Embassy. I'd never told her what Ferdy had said to me, partly because she'd asked me not to and partly because at mafia sessions everybody had been carefully keeping off that kind of subject. Even after the last great twin-battle, which had finished up with two bleeding noses and a black eye—Ferdy'd got distracted by Mrs Farquson-Colquhoun, who I don't suppose is really a nympho, but . . . anyway, the F-Qs have a villa on Mallorca and Mrs F-Q pretended she wanted to practise her holiday Spanish on Ferdy and it turned out to be mostly body-language and Ferdy was responding in kind and I was giggling away behind a pillar so we were *all* distracted when there was this colossal flare-up among the ravens . . . where was I? Yes, even at the mafia post-mortem we'd managed not to say anything about Juan and Ferdy coming from Matteo. Now, I don't know why—perhaps because of the way Mrs Dunnitt had laughed—I plunged in.

"I did ask Ferdy about the PDS," I began.

"I do not want to talk about that. If you wish, you can tell me whether you thought he told you the truth."

"Oh, yes! At least, I think what he told me was mostly true, but he left a bit out. He wouldn't say whether he was in the PDS, for instance. But he did tell me how his family got killed."

"Don't go on. I will accept that he may have told you some of the truth. But you see, whatever his justifications—and at a personal level they may be real and understandable—they cannot be enough."

"Can I ask you something else?"

"If you wish."

"Are we really enemies?"

"What are you talking about?"

"When you were explaining about the PDS—I don't know if you remember—you said something about the opera being run for the benefit of your enemies, only you declared a sort of truce. It wasn't quite like that, but . . ."

"I may have said something of the kind."

"But I don't feel like an enemy. I feel like an old, old friend."

She laughed again, but this time it was much more the kind of sound you'd have expected.

"That's the problem, or part of it," she said.

"I don't understand."

"Of course not. Your comfort, your safety, your sanity depend on your not understanding."

"So it's not my fault if I don't?" I said.

"I didn't say that. Let me tell you a story. For most of my life I have been a member of the Communist Party. A dedicated member. My husband was killed in Spain, and I thought—I still think—the sacrifice was worth while. I am only talking about my share of the sacrifice, my loss of him. I loved him very much, but I was prepared to lose him for the cause. Now, I am not a fool, and I am according to my lights honest, but for many years I believed what I needed to believe and I refused to believe what I could not afford to believe. I believed what I now know to be monstrous lies and disbelieved evident truths. I visited Russia several times and saw only what they wished me to see. They never had to tell me not to look or listen, because I knew what was expected of me. I have shaken hands with Stalin and felt nothing but the honour so great a man did me. I did not even have the excuse of other travellers, as I had taken the trouble to learn Russian and spoke it quite well. Once, late in the evening, a drunk young man started to tell me in the corner of a crowded room what was actually happening in the prisons and the camps.

I was furious. I shut him up. Next morning I denounced him to
our guide. He was never seen in Moscow again. I do not know
what became of him, but in dreams I have seen him, haggard
with hunger, one of a line of other men, pausing from his work
to spit blood onto the snow beside the ditch he is being forced to
dig."

I'd read *One Day in the Life*, so I knew what she was talking
about.

"You're not the first person I've told about this," she said.
"I'm like the Ancient Mariner, except that I've never done it at a
wedding. It is part of my penance. You see, I didn't come to
myself next week and realise that I had done something unforgivable—it took another twenty-seven years. I accepted the
show trials, I accepted the Ribbentrop Pact, I accepted the
invasion of Hungary. All that time I made myself blind and deaf.
I both knew and refused to know the truth. When my friends fell
away from the cause I would not forgive them. I felt they had
betrayed me and mankind. But now, if I believed in a God, I
would not expect Him to forgive me. It was my fault I did not
know, you see—much more clearly than your ignorance is your
fault."

She smiled at me like a sweet old lady who's never been
interested in anything except cats and gardening.

"Do you think we live in a just society, my dear?" she said.

"It could be worse."

"It could be a little worse. It could be like Matteo."

"Or Russia?"

"Or Russia—though Russia is a special case. They have, in a
sense, tried. We have not."

"And that's my fault too?"

"Collectively it's our fault. Your share of the blame is very
small—as yet. It will become more and more so long as you
refuse to let yourself see the injustice, or else see it and turn
away. But it is in your own interest to shut your eyes and ears,
just as I did. The easiest thing is simply not to know. Our

country, and others like it, is run with the prime object of making you and me comfortable. In the days of the cave-men we would have been the ones with places close to the fire. As it is, we are the ones who have the cottages in Wales and the Volvos and the private education for our children and the index-linked salaries and pensions. But we are not fools. And we have consciences. We can see that our privileges need to be justified. In the cave the place by the fire would have been ours because our father, or our husband, had the responsibility of leading the hunting-pack—that's still one form of justification. But of course we also have to persuade ourselves that it's not really all that cold among the families who huddle against the cave wall— and we do our best not to think about the people right outside, the babies being born with nothing to shelter them but a hole in the snow. Our own children will be born in the glow of the flames. By that we judge the comfort of the cave."

"You're talking about 'we'," I said. "Aren't 'we' your enemies?"

"My father was a successful tea-merchant. We lived in one of those big houses near the bottom of Ladbroke Grove. Until 1939 there were always at least three living-in servants. I was born quite close to the fire. I have crawled a little way and been pushed a little way towards the wall."

"Do you want me to begin to crawl too?"

She sighed.

"It is not for me to say. Only I will tell you this—suppose we lived in a tolerably just society and suppose I were young enough to have a daughter your age, I would be happy for her to be very much like you. But with the world as it is I should not be happy. I should want her much angrier, much more dis-contented and difficult, yes, much more painful.

"Finished? Admirable child. You will find that even in a liberated age the ability to work and listen at the same time is a great advantage to a woman. Now loosen the waist at least six inches and then—see that bit of silvery gauze on the end of the

rack?—tack that on at the shoulders—very loose—I want it to
float—and then you can try it on and we'll see how it looks
when you do your famous provocative strut . . ."

I can't say I saw the world with new eyes from then on. I felt a
bit ashamed about not haranguing Dad across the breakfast-
table about the cottage and the Volvo and his pension, but . . .
The only person I actually tried to talk to about Mrs Dunnitt
was Adam, and we weren't on the same wavelength, although
he goes on demos too and knows about things like the
Ribbentrop Pact and the invasion of Hungary. He was pretty
contemptuous. I couldn't seem to put over what Mrs Dunnitt
had put over to me, the actual *feel* of what it had been like to be
alive then and living through those things. That's the trouble
with all these exams we do—you begin to feel the world is full
of right answers, and the people in history must have been idiots
not to see them at the time.

But there was one moment when I actually found myself
looking at things in a Mrs Dunnitt kind of way. When I say
things, I mean the ravens. We had a special rehearsal with Elijah,
the week before the run-up week. They were sitting quietly on
the steps of the dais while Prue took Jake Laver through the
Elijah movements. The raven masks were lined out on the floor
in front of them, glossy black menacing beaks for pecking eyes
out with. I started by noticing what an incredibly grown-up face
Queenie Windsor had—round and soft and smug, so that it was
a bit of a shock to realise it wasn't at all childish. She would have
the same face when she was a mum, I thought, a dead
competent mum, running her house and family just the way she
wanted and whatever happened in the rest of the world no
business of hers unless it threatened her bubble of comfort—and
then she'd fight with utter ruthlessness to stop the bubble being
pricked. I wondered what her husband would be like—certainly
not a Conyers-Smith twin—she was too tough for them,
despite her look of softness. Nothing like Juan O'Grady, either,

though he was something different. If Queenie and the twins grew up into what Mrs Dunnitt called her enemies, they'd be the kind who fought her without understanding why. Juan would know. He was an extraordinarily conscious child—for instance, the twins were little male brutes because that was what they were, without having to think about it. Juan was what he had chosen to be—a bit less brutish than the twins, but much more male. A couple of times he'd even done a sort of parody of Ferdy's tiger-act at me. He knew what it was about. He'd be a real nuisance one day. But the twins seemed to think that the only serious difference between the sexes was that girls were less fun to punch.

I became aware of the strangeness of my own mood, hunched on the front pew, staring at the children as if they were tea-leaves in my cup of fortune. By the time they were old enough to take the shapes I seemed to see I would be almost as old as Mrs Dunnitt, my own life good as over, all its regrets set solid, like the dog's footprints in the bit of cement in the pavement outside Number 16. I watched Katie Drew. I remembered Mrs Slim at the casting session saying she was rather sweet. She seemed to me to be just twitchily eager to please and sure she wasn't going to. *She* might be more the twins' type . . . Mrs Conyers-Smith could have been a bit like Katie, once . . . it was interesting that Juan, half-absentmindedly as a manoeuvre in his feud with the twins, had chosen to protect Katie . . . Was she a bit of a leech, really? The sort who'd find somebody to look after her between breakdowns?

I must have shivered.

"You see ghosts?" whispered Ferdy, sitting beside me with his guitar across his knees.

"Sort of, I suppose. Well, future ghosts."

Quite serious, he took my right hand and moved it in the pattern of a cross over my chest.

"All right, ravens," called Prue in her fruity, jollying voice. "Masks on and into your places . . . now remember, all of you,

you've got to get up the steps Mr Slim's going to build . . . here.
They aren't there now, so tonight you've got to allow extra
time. I want you to stop for one whole bar when you reach the
edge of the dais . . . here . . . and then move on. That bar's your
step-climbing time. Ready, Elijah? Ready, Elsie and Ferdy? Last
verse of your solo, Elijah . . . Two, three . . ."

Jake sang,

> "All that Yahweh tells me I
> Obediently prophesy,
> And it happens by and by.
> But he never told me I
> In this desert hot and dry
>   Must die."

As the last note wailed on Ferdy began to pluck the jerky
rhythm of the raven dance. There was a racket of cawing from
the front vestry door and the first pair, flapping their wings,
strutted to the edge of the dais. Even under the ordinary church
lighting they looked amazingly sinister.

"Must die," sang Jake again. "Must die. I. Why?"

Chapter Six

For the dress rehearsals and the actual performances the children don't come direct to the church—they're split into groups and change into their costumes at different houses round the square, and get made up and so on, and then come streaming across. This means among other things that we don't have to cope with their ordinary clothes in the church, but of course we still have the problem of shoes—a hundred pairs of shoes and sandals, and even boots, and no matter what you tell them, half the children are too excited to do anything except kick them off the moment they're in the church, so that anyone going anywhere—and you're usually in a hurry and the church lights are out, of course—is apt to go sprawling or at least make a disastrous clatter. And then after each performance there's always a dozen smalls wandering miserably around clutching one shoe and looking for the other.

This year, I decided, there wasn't going to be any of that. There was going to be a *system*, and it was going to work. With Ferdy looking after my ravens I could be in the church before the cast arrived and see that every darned sandal, shoe and boot went somewhere sensible. The first dress rehearsal was my shoe rehearsal. And it was a shambles. The new arrangement simply confused everybody, and with only half the cast in there seemed to be more loose shoes lying around than ever. I was working myself into a Mum-like state of silent fury by the west door when Simon Laver came pushing against the current from inside the church and told me in his usual languid I'm-not-impressed voice that Mrs Slim couldn't find the sacristy key in any of the usual places so there wasn't anywhere to plug the electric xylophone in. Thankfully I left Simon in charge of the shoe problem, ran up the side-aisle and pushed my way into the front vestry. The clamour in there was appalling—for some reason that's always the main riot-centre, with too many over-excited smalls waiting too long for things to begin. I shoved through the mob to the far corner and managed to pull the table that stands there out enough to open the door behind it. I crawled under the table and into the dark. A couple of boisterous tribesmen came wriggling after me until I snarled at them and they went back. I picked my way down into the dark, cursing my idiocy for not having brought a torch to the rehearsal—I should have known I'd need one, somehow, somewhere.

The door in the vestry looks like a cupboard, and there's another just like it in the sacristy, with a sort of secret passage running between them, down steep winding steps and then under the main altar. I groped my way, stumbling among boxes of forgotten junk that had been stored there—broken altar-sconces, collections of out-of-date prayer-books, parts of antique vacuum-cleaners, even odd props from previous operas. I knew my way because I'd been down there with Mr Slim to see if there was anything any use this time. At last I reached the far steps, climbed them, got into the sacristy and turned on the light. When I opened the door into the church I found Mrs Slim standing there, pathetically clutching the lead to the xylophone.

"Doll, you're a miracle," she said.

I showed the xylophone man the socket and wandered out into the church. Absolutely suddenly, like being hit by a wave, I was flooded with joy. The same excitement that made the smalls in the vestry clamour and scuffle and throw pieces of chalk took hold of me. This was what I was in the opera for—nothing to do with producing art for its own sake, or embodying the ethos of the bourgeoisie, or making money for Onward's charities— this. I stood on the steps of the side-chapel and looked down the nave. The orchestra was just in front of me, tuning and twiddling, their faces lit by glow reflected from the lights on their music-stands. I saw Mum bowed over the Testori—she oughtn't to risk bringing it to rehearsals, of course, but she does. She was absorbed, lost, totally happy. The ordinary church lights were still on, but Mr Tolland was up in the back gallery fiddling with the stage lighting, so that suddenly one part of the church would be bathed in glare and all the other lights there would go dead as lamps in a painting. One of Jezebel's hand-maids (Veronica Drew, of course, exploiting things to draw attention to herself) went running down the centre aisle, trailing the green and silve gauze I'd unpicked for her. The air reeked with the smell of sawdust and half-dried paint. Mrs Dunnitt was striding about, clutching at passing children like the old witch in a fairy-tale, tugging at a robe, sticking a safety-pin into a waist-line, adding a great smear of make-up—her amateur assistants were always too timid with the stuff, she thought—or snarling at some trembling tot that even though this was only a rehearsal there was no question of doing the Baal-dance in grey school socks. I saw her grab Veronica and make her stand still while she finished her argument about the socks. The noise in the front vestry had risen till it was now like a henhouse at feeding-time. I saw Mrs Banks scurrying towards it as if she were a fire-engine whose pumps could squirt silence.

Oh, I love this, I thought. I love this. You don't have to be in it to be part of it. I'm never going to give it up, never. Tingling with the pleasure of it I began to make my way back towards the west door and the dreaded shoe problem. Mr Tolland was playing with his fire from heaven, so that the walls and pillars flickered with crimson waves of light. It made it feel as though the old church had come alive with a weird, electric life, like one of those luminous sea-creatures, so that it could be part of the opera too.

A bit over half-way down the centre aisle you cross another aisle, which runs from the main south door to the kitchen door.

Just beyond that we usually have a small extra stage—it's not very popular with the people in the front pews who've paid more to be there and then find themselves having to crane round to see things way behind them, but it does mean that the audience at the back get some of the action in close-up. Anyway, it's more fun if we're using the whole church and not doing everything stodgily up on the same main stage. When we did *Joseph* (my chief-slave year), Pharaoh's court, all in white except for their head-dresses, made their first entry up the centre aisle from the back of the church. As they came over the little back-stage Mr Tolland lit them from below, so that they looked like a religious procession going over a bridge, shining with inward whiteness in the dark of the church. It was magical. I was thinking of that moment, that shining entrance, as I edged round the stage to get to the west door. Then everything changed.

All I heard was what sounded like a car with a wonky engine going past, and then a scuffle at the south door. I turned and saw the ravens come bursting through. I ran round the back of the pews towards them, making shooing movements—they knew perfectly well they were supposed to come in through the west door like everyone else. Over their heads I could see something happening in the porch. Mr Talati seemed to be trying to get the outer doors shut. The ravens came rushing on as if they hadn't even seen me.

"What the hell do you think you're doing?" I screeched. "You know quite well . . . and where's Ferdy?"

"They've shot him," shouted one of the twins.

"They've shot him, they've shot him!" clamoured the others. Katie Drew was sobbing. Even then I couldn't grasp what was up. I just grabbed the nearest child and almost threw her towards the back vestry.

"Get your masks, anyway," I snapped. "We'll sort it out . . ."

I shoved two more. The others scrambled past. Automatically I counted them—Melissa, twin, Queenie, Katie, Camilla, twin—six. I was just about to spin round to look for Juan when the shock of understanding gripped me and I found myself turning slowly, icily, the way you move when you've woken from a nightmare but you aren't yet really sure you're safe in your own bed and there's nothing terrifying in the room. The noise in the church had hardly changed—the chatter and scurry of children and Mr Slim banging a few last tacks into his stage carpet and the orchestra still tweeting and plonking, but as I turned I felt a stillness moving inwards, like a cold draught, from the south door.

Two men in denims were striding round the back of the pews towards me. They were quite young—they could easily have been a couple of Marco's friends. One of them had a gun crooked on his right arm—the sort with its magazine curving upwards. The other had a pistol. They weren't running, but hurrying with tremendous leggy strides, and it was hardly a second before they reached me. Without thinking what I was doing I tried to stand in their way, croaking, "He isn't here! He isn't here!" Behind me a door slammed.

The men hardly looked at me, but as he passed the one with the pistol grabbed my right wrist, twisting it behind my back and pushing me towards the vestry. The door was shut.

"Open!" he growled.

I scrabbled at the handle with my left hand but the door wouldn't move. The man must have thought I was holding things up on purpose, because he wrenched my arm up till I screamed and at the same time shoved me against the door like a battering ram. It gave with a rush as the children who'd been holding it from the far side sprawled back. I would have fallen straight in if the man hadn't been holding my arm. The stillness in the vestry—there were forty or fifty children in there who'd normally have been chattering and jostling like a roost of starlings—was more of a shock than screams would have been. They knew. They understood. They were terrified too.

But I could feel the man who was holding me hesitate. He couldn't have been expecting a problem like this—all those kids

in fancy dress and the ravens scattered among them. They'd
actually got their masks on, too. I'd only told them to because
I'd still been thinking about getting things set up for the entrance
procession but I suppose they thought my order had been part of
some instant plan to thwart these men. Eyes stared at us, dull
with fright. The black beaks bobbed above the faces. There was
a noise of tearing paper.

"He isn't here!" I said loudly. "He didn't come! Look! Only
six ravens—you can count them!"

"Quiet," growled the man who was holding me.

I saw the children's eyes widen. Then I felt something cold
against my temple.

"Hear me!" said the man in a loud voice. "Do what I tell you
and no one will be hurt. Do anything else and I shoot this lady.
Understand? Now, one at a time you'll all go out and sit on the
benches in the church. Not the blackbirds. They stay here. OK?
Move!"

His accent was American—almost too American to be true,
as if he was putting it on. The children hesitated, stuck where
they were with fright.

"Go on," I managed to whisper. "Amy, you go first. Do
what he says."

Clutching her cardboard-tipped spear Amy Blow edged past.
The man pulled me to one side so that now I could see his friend
standing just outside the door with his gun raised and ready in
case there was some kind of rush from the nave. The children
filed out in silence. I was terrified in case some little thug should
have a dream of comic-strip glory and make a snatch at the gun
as he went by, but it didn't happen. As the last of them was
going the man swung me back and gave me a push towards the
ravens who were standing in a huddle over by the wardrobe,
black and bedraggled, almost like real birds.

"Bring me the O'Grady kid," he said.

"He isn't here, I tell you!"

He sighed.

"OK," he said. "Bring me the kids, one at a time. Take off the headpieces."

I crossed the room, lifted off Camilla's mask and put it in her hands. The man nodded and gestured with his gun for her to go and sit outside and for me to send him another raven. I could hear now that the whole church had gone dead quiet. Next was one of the twins, next Katie, next the other twin . . .

"Hey! What you doing?" snarled the man. He shoved the twin back towards me so hard that he sent him sprawling. There was a gabble of Spanish between him and the other man, who strode out of sight. A few seconds later he was shepherding the ravens back into the room. Believe it or not they had their masks on again. The first man's face changed. He took a deep breath, let it out again and stared hard at me. His pistol seemed to twitch in his hand. My heart slammed.

"They're twins!" I heard myself shouting. "Identical twins! Ravens, take your masks off, all of you, for God's sake!"

I couldn't take my eyes off the pistol. It went down again and I was shuddering. The huge beaks tilted and rose as the children lifted their masks clear, and I pushed them into line—all I cared about was making the man see we hadn't been messing him around. I stood the twins side by side so that he could see how alike they were. As I went back to his side I noticed a pile of shoes against the far wall—according to my system they should have been on the shelves I'd specially cleared of hymn-books for them, but now . . . under the shoes was a crumpled mess of shiny black paper.

If the man had been watching me he must have seen my face change, but he was frowning at the twins. For the first time I could sense uncertainty, a loss of control, his own drive and purpose stumbling. I felt even more frightened. Now he might do anything.

With his free hand he pointed at Katie.

"You," he said. "How many blackbirds in this play?"

Katie, of course, broke into gulps of sobbing.

"We're ravens, not blackbirds," said Queenie in a calm, chilly voice. "There's just six of us, that's all."

"Where's the O'Grady kid?" said the man.

The children looked at each other. It was extraordinary—as though they'd suddenly stumbled into the middle of a game whose rules they knew. I remembered their huddle by the wardrobe—they'd have had time for a quick whisper. Oh, God, I thought, don't let them try anything! They mimed stupidity, bafflement.

"Don't try that, you little bastards," said the man. "I'm not joking. See this here? It's a gun, a real gun. Real bullets. You want me to blow your leg off, so you can't ever walk again? No? Well you tell me where's Juan O'Grady!"

"Oh, you mean *One*!" said Queenie.

"Uh?"

"One. He doesn't like to be called Jew Ann and One's easier than Hwaan."

"OK, OK. Where is he?"

"Not here. He didn't come," said Queenie.

She sounded as though she was lying—perhaps she meant to. At any rate the man's eyes fell on the vestment wardrobe and he said something over his shoulder in Spanish. The other man strode across and wrenched at the wardrobe door. Onward keeps it locked because apparently there are nuts around who have a kink about choir-vestments and break into churches and steal them. I was opening my mouth to say so when the man turned his gun round and smashed hard at the lock with its butt. Modern church furniture tends to be pretty flimsy, but the wardrobe was old and solid and all the man achieved was a tremendous banging and booming.

"The key?" snapped the man with the pistol. "Where's the goddam key?"

"I don't know," I gabbled. "Really I don't. He keeps it locked. Always locked. In the sacristy, I expect—the key."

More Spanish, angry and frightened. Another man appeared at

the door and asked a question in a soft, calm voice. The first man
explained, still in Spanish, but I could see he was saying
something about the twins. I guessed he thought we'd been
working some kind of conjuring trick, using their likeness to
smuggle Juan out of the vestry by making it seem that there was
one more or one less raven than there ought to be.

The new man nodded and came into the room, bringing with
him a curious kind of calm—everything was still terrifying and
dangerous, but it didn't seem to be for him. He was shorter than
the others and rather plump, with a shiny bald forehead and a
heavy black beard. He didn't look particularly like Ferdy, but he
could easily have been a close relation—they had a sort of family
feel in common. He carried a pistol in his right hand. He glanced
at me and rejected me, then hunkered down in front of the line
of children.

"You listen, kids," he said. "We are friends. We do not wish
to hurt you, understand?"

They stared at him. His accent was very foreign, a sort of
wheedling drawl, but the actual English was fairly good.

"We do not wish to hurt any person," he went on. "Not Juan
O'Grady, even. We take him away because bad men in his
country—our country also—keep our friends in terrible prisons.
Understand? When they give us back our friends, we give them
back Juan. OK? Nobody hurt, nobody at all, and our friends are
free from their terrible prison. So where is the boy? We have
been watching. We know he comes always to the play."

"Not always," said Queenie. "He's spare—in case one of us is
ill. He almost wasn't in the opera at all, because we were full
up."

(It's extraordinary the way children learn things they're
supposed to know nothing about. I only realised afterwards, of
course.)

"I think he came tonight," said the man. "Why was his guard
here if he was not coming?"

"Ferdy?" said Queenie. "Oh, he has to come, whatever

happens. He plays the guitar for the raven dance, don't you see?"

The man asked a question in Spanish and the first man hesitated and answered. I could feel time slithering away. This couldn't go on. The church wasn't an island right out in space, for God's sake—it was in the middle of London, there were police, friends . . . Queenie had managed to sound just right, as though she was being patient with a slightly thick adult. It happened to be true that Juan had had flu a fortnight before and had missed a rehearsal, but Ferdy had still come to play for the raven dance. It could have been true tonight . . .

"We were watching the embassy," said the man in a less friendly voice. "The boy came OK."

"Oh yes," said Queenie. "He came to the *house*. But he got the sulks because he wasn't wanted tonight. I expect he's still there—or he's made his chauffeur take him home."

I could hear my heart clumping. Believe her, believe her, I prayed. I couldn't read his face. He shrugged, gave Queenie a sour little smile then swung like a pouncing cat on Katie Drew.

"Where is this boy?" he hissed.

"You shot him, you shot him," sobbed Katie.

She tried to back away but he grabbed her wrist.

"The boy," he said. "The O'Grady kid."

"Don't know! Go away! Why did you shoot him? Why did you shoot him?"

Katie began to scream, working herself into spasms of total terror, staggering around when the man let her go. I knelt, caught her and hugged her tight, but still she screamed. Her body was all hard knots like twisted rubber, jerking into each scream, almost too strong to hold. I looked up. The man with the beard had risen and was talking with the other two by the door. I couldn't hear a word through Katie's screams, but the first man was arguing and gesturing towards the nave with his pistol. The second man was looking anxious, almost panicky. The man with the beard at last nodded and led them away.

"They're going," I whispered into Katie's ear. "It's all right. They're going away. They're going."

Her screams died into gulps and shudders. I rose to my feet, lifting her with me and settling her head against my shoulder. Her arms closed round my neck like hard straps. I moved on tip-toe to the door and up by the font until I was standing at the edge of the shadow under the gallery. The whole church was quite still, everybody sitting in pews but craning round towards the south door where the three men stood. Two of them I could see were desperate to be off, but the man with the beard seemed in no hurry. He turned to the silent church and raised his pistol over his head, like an umpire starting a race.

"OK," he called. "Now we go. But you will remember us, you rich people, you friends of the fascist criminal Blick. We, the Movement of Third April, will . . ."

He froze. Outside the church there was a noise. I'd heard it earlier, but now I knew what it was it didn't sound a bit like a car with a wonky engine. The man with the machine-gun slipped into the porch. Now I heard the whang whang whang of a police siren, belting closer, with another beyond it. Enormously loud from the porch a gun rattled off a burst of fire, followed by a deeper boom as the outer door slammed. The inner doors swung open with a crash and a woman burst through, blue-denimed like the rest of them. She spoke hurriedly to the man with the beard, gesturing with a machine-gun as she did so. I could only see her from the back. She was taller than the man with the beard and her hair was done into hundreds of tiny plaits with beads at the end. The man with the beard handed his pistol to the girl, took her machine-gun from her and climbed onto the pew by the door, pointing the gun out towards us.

"OK," he said, still as calmly as if we were all just practising some kind of fire-drill. "You will all sit on the benches. You will not move. If any person does what we do not want, we will shoot. We will shoot until you all are dead. Understand? Now one adult will come with me to show me all the doors of this church, to lock them. Quick!"

I saw Mr Slim getting to his feet.

"Come on," I whispered, and led the six ravens off to join the others in the pews. Outside more and more sirens—police cars or fire-engines or ambulances—closed in.

Chapter Seven

They never meant to take us hostages, of course. You have to remember this, because it helps explain a lot of what happened afterwards—really they weren't any readier than we were and had to make everything up as they went along. When it was all over it turned out that they'd been watching our routine for weeks and were planning to snatch Juan as he got out of the embassy Rolls at the church, but they hadn't realised that that Monday was the first dress rehearsal. The Rolls came early and went to Mrs Fearon's house, where the ravens were changing. The bandits turned up and hung around. When the children started streaming across to the church they decided to try and spot Juan and snatch him then, but the ravens came out of Mrs Fearon's in a tight little bunch—all in black, remember, with flapping great wings, and the lamplight is pretty patchy round the square—and they'd only guessed Juan might be among them because Ferdy was with them. No one knows quite what happened next, but anyway they were out on the pavement when Ferdy spotted them and drew his gun. Then there was shooting and the ravens had time to get into the church, leaving Ferdy lying in the gutter. Mr Talati hadn't quite managed to get the door shut before the three men followed them in. The girl had stayed to guard their car outside. When the first police had turned up she'd fired a burst at it and then joined her friends.

And why hadn't we all—or as many of us as possible—slipped out of the other doors? It's easy to say that now, and of course it would have worked, but the shooting had been *outside*, remember, all in the dark. Nobody could know that there weren't lots of people waiting out there with guns. It wasn't anything to do with me, but I do see that to all the adults in charge it must have seemed far, far safer to keep everyone quiet where they were—in the light, under control—than let them rush panicking out into the dark.

The pews were incredibly uncomfortable. I don't mean that there was anything different about them, though during the past weeks I must have sat through almost fifty hours of rehearsal without noticing that they were anything except ordinary shiny hard wood. The difference was in me. I was so screwed up with fright—the fright of what had happened already and the other fright of moving even a finger in case I started the men shooting —that all my muscles ached with stillness. It was like when you're standing on a ladder a bit further up than you're happy with—after a while you find that muscles which you aren't even using have gone tense, as if they were trying to grow an extra hand to hold on with. I kept looking at my watch. Time hardly seemed to move at all. The bandits—I'll call them that, though it isn't really fair, but I've got to have a word for them—the bandits had herded us all into the front pews. At first one of them stood in front of us on the dais with his gun on his arm, not really watching us but peering up into the darkness beyond us; but after about twenty minutes they rigged up a different system. They lugged out from the rack in the front vestry five of the altar frontals which Onward keeps there. These are big lengths of embroidered cloth, about ten feet long and four feet wide, stretched on light frames. There are different colours for different church fasts and seasons and festivals. Onward says that some of the Victorian ones are museum pieces, but the bandits didn't mind about that. They stuck holes in them so that they could lash them together into a sort of hide half-way down the centre aisle, behind us all, open our end but closed off at the back and sides. I was so stupid with shock and fear that it took me some time to realise what the point was, even after the bandit who'd been watching us from the stage went down and posted himself there, but I got it in the end. There were just four bandits, you see—far too few to guard the church like defenders in a siege. Their only defence was the threat that they would do something to us before the people outside could prevent them, and quite soon the army, or the special police experts, would arrive and get ladders up to the church windows and be able to shoot any bandits they could see. Now they wouldn't be able to see the one in the hide—he was screened from the side windows by the hide itself and from the big east window by Jezebel's tower and so on, filling the chancel arch. I suppose the army marksmen could have riddled the hide with bullets from all sides, but they still couldn't be sure of getting him before he'd started killing us. It would have been a perfectly hideous risk to take. So while we sat there, and while one bandit watched us from the hide with his gun cocked and ready, there wasn't anything much the people on the outside dared do.

But there wasn't much the bandits dared do either—in fact I didn't see how either side could risk shifting the balance. I tried to remember about the siege in the Iranian Embassy in the spring. How long had that gone on for? Days, wasn't it? Six days? That'd be ghastly . . . and what about the opera, for heaven's sake? Saturday and Sunday were the actual performances, and we simply had to have at least two more dress rehearsals before . . . I knew it was ridiculous to worry about that—what did it matter the opera being ruined provided we all got out safe? But I couldn't help it. Under all my fears a part of my mind kept nagging away at that.

I was still clutching Katie Drew—or rather she was clutching me, though she'd fallen deep asleep and was only shuddering a little in her dreams. Beyond her sat Queenie Windsor, still looking quite calm, even a bit bored. It was slowly sinking into my mind that but for the bad luck of the bandit leader wanting to make his speech and the police cars coming a bit too soon, Queenie would have got rid of the bandits single-handed. It was

quite impossible to tell from her face whether she'd any idea
what she'd almost brought off or how close a call it had been.
Perhaps she was screaming with disappointment inside, but for
all I could see she could have forgotten about the whole thing.
Perhaps even while she was doing it she hadn't properly grasped
what she was up to; even so she had quite definitely taken
charge. I thought, if ever we get out of this I'm going to see that
Mum and the others realise.

A vague sort of bustle and muttering began, over towards the
south door, but it was hidden from where I sat by the hide, and
in any case when we craned round the bandit sitting there
gestured to us angrily to face forward. But now a hand touched
my shoulder. I looked round and saw it was Mr Slim, leaning
over from the side-aisle. He beckoned. When I tried to get up
Katie began to whimper in her sleep and her hug tightened
round my neck, but then Queenie slipped an arm round Katie's
shoulder and gently heaved her the other way, close against her
own body. I smiled at her but she only nodded, very serious and
confident. The whimpers dwindled and I edged past Melissa and
Camilla out into the aisle.

Mr Slim led me back to where the bearded bandit was
waiting.

"Sorry, Doll," he whispered. "They wanted one of the
children. I tried to insist it had to be an adult. Do you mind
being the compromise?"

"What for?"

"They want me to go and parley with the police, but they've
got to have one of us to hold visibly at gun-point while I'm
talking. It should be perfectly safe."

"I don't mind. I'm getting used to it."

He looked blank. I realised that of course he had no idea what
had happened in the back vestry. The bandit waved impatiently
to us and strode towards the south door. As we followed I
whispered, "There are only six ravens. Pass it on."

"I know," whispered Mr Slim. "Do the other ravens?"

I was baffled but hadn't time to think about it before the bandit turned, frowning, beckoned us forward and marched us in front of him. We'd kept our voices right down, but the church is like that—whispers seem to float through it, though you can't pick out the actual words—it can be absolutely maddening at rehearsals when mums begin chatting in the back pews.

The girl was waiting at the door. She and Mr Slim and the bearded man started an argument in Spanish. She seemed angry and excited, the man calm as ever. Mr Slim spoke slowly and quietly but used his hands more than he would have if he'd been speaking English. His face was the colour of stale bread. I remembered what Adam had told me about him having a not-quite heart-attack. The girl . . .

I hadn't really looked at her before. When she'd burst into the church to tell Danny the police were coming I'd just seen her wild look and the way she did her hair. Now I couldn't stop staring at her. She was quite extraordinary—coloured more golden than coffee, fairly tall, very slim legs and hips and waist, but then a forty-four bust I should think and shoulders like a man's and a neck like a carthorse's, all smooth muscle but carrying a little oval head with neat little features framed by those black plaits with beads at the end. She would have looked a bit mad even in her sleep, but now, as she got wilder and wilder arguing with Mr Slim, she looked absolutely nutters. Suddenly my stomach went all small—*she* was going to hold me at gun-point while Mr Slim and the bearded man talked with the people outside. Of course. Anyone could see that she really might shoot if the bandits didn't get what they wanted . . . As the argument ended she turned to me. Her eyes glittered. I guessed she'd hopped herself up to the raid with drugs and my stomach grew smaller still.

In fact it wasn't too bad. The south door porch is beneath the tower, so it's quite a big space. On the street side there's a pair of big wooden doors painted red inside and out, and between the porch and the nave there's a double set of swing-doors, like an air-lock, covered with green baize. The bandits had hooked these open. Now they stood me under the light in the middle of the porch and told Mr Slim to go to the outer doors. The man and the girl went to the far corners of the porch so that when Mr Slim opened the doors all anyone on the outside could see was one gun pointing straight at me and only a bit of the man's face and his hand holding a pistol pointing at Mr Slim.

The moment the doors were open light blazed in. The porch light became faint and yellow compared with the dead white of the floodlight beyond. I could hear the steady drum of a generator. The floodlight wasn't shining straight into the porch but still the pavement outside seemed bright as day—not at all like day, though, because I could sense the darkness further out. It had begun to rain, glittering down through the glare. Mr Slim stepped two paces out onto the pavement and waited. He was wearing his old green jersey, covered with paint-smears and full of holes, and at once that and his hair began to glisten with rain-drops.

A man in a pale raincoat came out of the whiteness and offered him a brolly. Mr Slim hesitated and looked over his shoulder. "OK," called the bearded bandit. "Stand so I am seeing two men." Mr Slim put the brolly up and turned sideways and the other man moved round to face him. They stood and talked, black against the brightness, which cast their shadows criss-cross on the pavement as if they'd been players in a floodlit football match. Mr Slim spoke slowly and loudly but I was too far back to catch much. The bearded man must have been able to get most of it, because twice he called out in Spanish and once he made Mr Slim come right back into the porch for a conference. It all seemed to take ages, but I don't remember much actually happening. I didn't even think very much, not sensible thoughts in a proper order. I kept trying not to look at the girl, because I was so afraid of her—far more than I was of any of the men. I stared at Mr Slim and the man in the raincoat, but I began to ache with the thought of the soft wet night beyond the floodlights, and the warm rooms, and people living among their families where everything was ordinary. It struck me that they might even have the telly on and be watching from the outside the same scene that I was watching from the porch, the way we'd all done during the Iranian Embassy siege, watching it as if it were almost a play. And it was, sort of. Gestures, Mrs Dunnitt had said. I was part of the play, but I wasn't really an actor—more like a prop, for the real actors to make their gestures with. If they killed me it would still be only a gesture. If they killed a church full of children stone dead it would be quite a big gesture, wouldn't it?

Suddenly the man with the beard called out, "Finish! Finish now!"

Mr Slim said a few more words, handed the umbrella over and came in. The girl swung her gun away from me and pointed it out at the night while Mr Slim and the other bandit slammed the doors shut and bolted them. At once Mr Slim turned to the man and began to argue in Spanish. Though he kept his voice even I could hear that he was angry and upset. The man made a gesture to cut him short, but he went on. Suddenly the girl stepped across in front of me, swung her arm and hit him with her open palm across the side of the head. The blow made a loud smack like a handclap. Mr Slim staggered. His mouth worked but no words came. The girl was swinging her arm to hit him again, but I must have caught it—at any rate I found myself clinging to it and shouting, "Don't! Don't! He's got a bad heart!"

The man, who had done nothing to stop her, shook his head gently at her. She lowered her arm and I let go.

"Too bad," said the man. "Now you go with him and sit on the benches."

Mr Slim didn't move. He was swaying where he stood, still with his mouth open as he dragged for air through it. I put my arm round his waist and drew his wrist over my shoulder and led him back into the nave. The first few steps it was like the night when Adam's awful friend Corny got blind drunk and we walked him back to Putney, but then I felt Mr Slim's pace strengthen and he began to carry his own weight. Mrs Slim was working her way out of the pews, ignoring the man in the hide who was calling to her to sit down. She came down the side-aisle looking desperately anxious. She must have heard me shouting.

"I'll do, darling," said Mr Slim. "Just a twinge. Got my pills?"

"In my bag. Thank you, Doll. I'll take him now."

She led him back to her pew. I followed. I was going to my place with the ravens, but as soon as I reached a point where the man in the hide could see me he swung his gun at me and barked at me to sit down. I could feel the children's fright, hovering above the pews like mist over a marsh, so I just squeezed myself down into the nearest space. Mrs Dunnitt made room for me by scooping her pile of spare costume-stuffs off the seat and under the pew in front.

"Well done," she whispered.

I couldn't stop quivering. The church seemed extra cold. After a while Mrs Dunnitt pulled a length of blanket out of her bundle and wrapped it round my shoulders. It must have made me look like one of the tribesmen, but I didn't feel any warmer. It was as though I was getting flu, but of course I wasn't really ill. Shock, they call it on the radio. "Five people were taken to hospital and treated for shock." Poor softies, I suppose I always thought, but now it was me and I couldn't help it.

I could though. Just knowing what it was made a difference. Though I still felt feeble and shivery I stopped being so sorry for myself and began thinking of myself as some other girl and despising her a little—the same way I guessed Queenie half-despised Katie Drew, even while she was comforting her. That made me aware of Mrs Dunnitt, sitting bolt up beside me, alert as a terrier. Easy for her, I thought, she's on these people's side. She's watching a game and her team's winning. Then I remembered her whisper, and the blanket, and her voice when she'd told me, weeks before, about the young man she'd denounced in Moscow, and what I'd said about her feeling like an old, old friend. You give your friends the breaks. Adam had said that when I'd bawled him out about Corny spoiling the evening by getting plastered just when the party was warming up. Even so, I decided I'd better be careful what I said to Mrs Dunnitt. I couldn't actually be sure she was on our side, either.

Time slowed right down again. The minutes ached away. When at last something started to happen I found myself watching as though it was the most interesting thing in the world, even though it was only Mr Tolland putting a ladder up to one of the south aisle windows and climbing up it, like a bear climbing a pole. He has the biggest bum you ever saw. Those windows start about twelve feet from the ground, each of them just a single slit, filled with plain glass leaded in diamond patterns and going up to a pointed arch. Mr Tolland tilted the bottom panel of the window open, took a pair of pliers out of his hip pocket and wrenched for a while at the wire mesh which is there to stop the windows being smashed by nuts or drunks chucking stones. One of the bandits was holding the bottom of the ladder for him, and after a bit I realised this was the man who had been guarding us from the hide. Carefully I peeped round to see who was there now.

It was the girl. She was standing with her right hand on her hip and her left foot planted a little forward. Her face was set like a mask and she stared out over our heads. It was a pose, an attitude struck on purpose, as if she'd been modelling for a photograph—guerrilla chic, I thought, but I expect in her own mind she was posing for the statue of liberation they were going to put up in the main square of San Matteo. Though I thought she hadn't been looking anywhere near me she seemed to catch my eye. She stared for a moment, but didn't say anything and fell back into her pose. Suddenly she shook her head, like a horse pestered with flies, so that the plaits flew out all round her and the beads rattled as they whirled and settled. The noise made the

children turn, and she did it again for their benefit, a deliberate
signal of danger, like the rattle of a snake when the cameraman
gets too close. The children stirred and muttered at the sound,
and Mrs Dunnitt whispered in my ear, "That woman is not
me—she is the daughter of my ideas."

She sounded as though she was at a play and just whispering a
comment on one of the actors to her friend in the next seat.

"Look this way, please," called the bearded man.

We all turned. He was standing in the centre of the stage. He
smiled approvingly at us and began to look up over our heads, as
though he was interested in the church architecture.

"These lights," he said. "The lights for the play—they are
working?"

"Yes," called Mr Tolland over his shoulder. He was standing
at the bottom of the ladder now, holding it for the bandit who
was peeping cautiously out over the sill as though he expected
someone to take a pot-shot at him from the road.

"OK," said the bearded man. "Let me have light on this place
where I stand."

Mr Tolland left the ladder and lumbered away. I heard him
climbing the gallery stairs, and then the whole stage area began
to glow as he brought the main floods slowly up until they were
so bright that we seemed to be sitting in dimness and gazing into
a glaring block of light. The bearded man moved around the
stage, nodding to himself. Though he seemed quite casual and
unhurried I had a definite feeling that he was excited about
something new, something different from the straight tension of
the adventure he was involved in. He went back to the middle of
the stage and pointed to either side of him.

"Not here," he called. "Not here. This centre part only."

The block of light shrank and became more intense as Mr
Tolland lowered the side-stage floods and brought up the centre
spotlight where Elijah was supposed to stand when he called
down fire from heaven. The bearded man nodded, tucked his
pistol into his belt and stepped into the centre of the light. He

spread his arms, palms forward, in a gesture of peace and friend-
ship, and smiled. His eyes and his teeth glittered in the fierce
light.

"I am very sorry we discomfort you," he said. "We hope it is
not for long—perhaps only this night. With Mr Slim I have
arranged that food will come, and blankets. Also I have told all
your families that you are quite safe, and no one is hurt, and no
one will be hurt if you do all we say. OK?

"Now I will tell you why we are doing all this. First I will say
that my name is Danny. I am not a criminal. In my own
country, which is called Matteo, I am a schoolteacher. I teach
especially the drama, just like you are making here. I am most
interested in this play you do, you know. I wish I could be in my
own country, doing things like this with the children. But it is
not possible. In Matteo nothing like this is possible.

"I wish you to imagine in your minds what it is to live in
Matteo. Imagine one day you come home from your school and
there is your mother, weeping, and she tells you that the police
have come and they beat your father and take him away because
he was seen to talk with a man who the police say is an enemy of
the government. But still you have your mother, and soon
perhaps the police will let your father go.

"But imagine your friend comes home and there is nobody
waiting. Father and mother both gone, and neighbours so afraid
that they shut the door in the face of your friend.

"Now imagine me, your schoolteacher. What do I do in such
a country? Must I teach only what the government and the
soldiers say, and when one of my pupils is one day missing,
must I hunch the shoulders and ask no questions? For yes, even
children they take away to their terrible prisons. Everyone must
be afraid is their argument. If a brave man is not afraid for
himself, then they will make him afraid for his children. This is
how it is in Matteo.

"So I am your schoolteacher—what do you wish that I do?
You wish me to fight, of course, so that these things cease from

happening. I think so. I stop teaching children—which is all I truly wish to do—and I begin to fight. It is difficult. The government is strong. They have the American tanks and guns and planes. They have the police and the soldiers. They have the money to pay many, many spies. We—I and my friends—are so few. Of course, all people wish this bad government to end, but only few have courage to fight. We do not win, not yet. We have a few little victories, but many defeats. Some of my friends the soldiers kill. Some they catch and take to their prisons and their camps of torture. These brave women and men, who fight for justice and for liberty, the soldiers keep in dark little holes in the ground, or in stinking huts in the hot desert, forty people in one small hut, no water, no air, so they go mad.

"I see you understand what men we fight. I see it in your good young faces . . ."

(He couldn't have seen a thing, actually, with that spotlight glaring at him.)

". . . I see you wish like me for the terrible prisons to be torn down, for my friends to come out of the dark holes, out of the fiery desert camps, for all the people to be no more afraid. Our nations, they are far apart. In the school where I was teacher the children are just at their morning lesson—so far apart. But liberty is not far apart. If in Matteo liberty is dead, in England she dies a little also. Liberty is one thing. The friends of liberty are one family. You are her friends, so you are my sisters and my brothers. Together we must fight the friends of fear.

"So now, what do we do? I tell you, we come to find one boy, Juan O'Grady is his name. I know of him no good, no bad, but of his family I know a lot of bad. It is his family put my friends in their prisons. Our idea is we take this boy—we never hurt him, of course—and we tell his family we do not give him back before they set our friends free from the prisons.

"Well, this boy is not here, it seems. And your police have entrapped us here with you. We cannot say to the police, Very sorry—we surrender, for then they will put us in prison and in

Matteo liberty will die a little more. So we endeavour to come to arrangement. We say to them we will keep you here until they give us certain things—an aeroplane and a little money and a promise that they will publish in the papers and on the radio certain true stories we tell them, saying what happens in Matteo.

"Of course your police do not at once agree, but in a little time they will do what we ask. Then you will go home. But now, my sisters and my brothers, you must do everything we ask. You must help us, because you are helping liberty not to die. Sit quiet. Be good. Make no trouble. When the food come you will eat, and soon after you will sleep. That is all."

He stayed where he was, under the spotlight. In fact he had hardly moved a muscle while he was speaking, but still he had really put it over. I don't mean I thought he was *right*—I remembered how he had let the girl hit Mr Slim in the porch —but I thought differently about him now. I was sure he believed that the people he was fighting were as bad as he said they were. And in another way, in a show-biz way—those glittering eyes, that stillness—he had been pretty impressive too. I wondered what the children made of it all.

While he was still standing there, enjoying the spotlight like a cat enjoying a patch of sunlight, a hand rose over on the far side. I only saw it, faint in the gloom, when he glanced that way and nodded.

"Why did you shoot Ferdy?" said Queenie Windsor's unmistakable chill voice. The children stirred, nervous again, but Danny—I'll call him that from now on—nodded.

"The guard?" he said.

"Yes."

He nodded again, considering. A change came over him. His skin went greeny yellow, his eye-sockets darkened into shadowy pits, and the lips in the middle of his beard lost their redness and turned almost black.

"Idiot," whispered Mrs Dunnitt.

For a moment I couldn't think what she meant, but then I

realised she must be talking about Mr Tolland. He'd brought up
the green spot he'd put there for when Jezebel orders the soldiers
out to massacre the prophets of Yahweh. Probably he couldn't
resist the temptation just to see what it looked like and he only
kept it on for a couple of seconds, but the effect was amazingly
sinister. I doubt if Danny even noticed.

"You see, this is war," he said. "Your fathers, or your grand-
fathers, fought a war against the Germans. They also fought for
liberty. Because of their fighting you are living now in a free
country. You are not slaves. But when they fight, when they
point their gun at a German, they cannot say 'Perhaps that is a
good man, a friend of peace, a friend of liberty.' They must pull
the trigger and kill the man because he is a soldier of the evil
things they fight. That is what we must do also, who fight for
liberty. Understand?"

Another hand rose near the front.

"Can we talk?" said a voice.

"If you do not make a loud noise," said Danny. "Yes?"

"Can we sing?" said someone else.

"If it is quiet, a little singing. Perhaps you practise for your
play. Yes?"

This time it was a tribesman in the pew right in front of me. I
heard Mrs Dunnitt suck in her breath with irritation.

"Can I go to the loo, please?"

Several other hands rose, of course, asking the same question.
Danny hesitated and asked a question in Spanish. Mr Slim
answered. More Spanish, and footsteps over by the north door,
where the kitchen and the loo are.

"OK," said Danny. "One at a time only. You ask first."

The tribesman started to scramble out. As soon as I saw who
it was I understood Mrs Dunnitt's mutter. That sort of reaction
is normal among the mafia whenever Veronica Drew's name
crops up. Pink and grinning under her stripy headscarf she
scampered away down the side-aisle. I thought of her, only an
hour ago, drawing attention to herself just the same way,

trailing green and silver gauzes . . . inside me I felt a jolt of shock, of danger. Veronica wasn't a tribesman. She was one of Jezebel's handmaids.

"Don't stare," whispered Mrs Dunnitt.

It was too late. The handmaids in their brilliant gauzes were sitting two pews in front of us. Third along was a child in green and silver. I could just see the side of the face. Even by Mrs Dunnitt's standards the make-up was amazing.

Chapter Eight

The children were singing, just for something to do—
> He's the king in the middle,
> He's the king in a muddle,
> In a muddle in the middle
> In the middle in a muddle,
> What'll he do?
> What'll he do?
> What'll he do?

It sounded marvellous partly because they were keeping the volume down the way Danny had told them and partly because the smalls, who always muddy the notes a bit, were mostly asleep, laid out in a row down the north side-aisle. Even when Bill's written a simple tune everyone can belt out, he always puts in some tricky parts for the good singers—we call them the boobiddydoops because that was the noise we actually had to make for one song one year. Now, with the balance altered and everybody singing pianissimo, the boobiddydoops had an absolute field day, and you could really hear why Bill had bothered to put them in at all, and even why some of the music simply had to be as difficult as he made it. I craned round to see where he'd got to.

(After Danny's speech the bandits had herded all the adults into the two pews close in front of the hide on the right side, and they'd kept a pretty tight check on us even after they'd let the children relax a bit. But by the time we'd all fed—somebody must have gone to the Kentucky Fried and ordered a hundred and fifty portions—and got the smalls through the loo and bedded down, they'd found they couldn't organise much of that sort of thing without our help, which meant a bit of give and take, so now we were allowed to talk too, and shuffle our places round, and so on.)

Bill was at the inside end of the last pew, talking to Toby. I knew it had to be something about music because Toby was moving his fingers in little rhythmic twitches and Bill was nodding an imaginary beat with his head. When the children reached the chorus again he started to beat a different time with his hand and his lips moved as if he was joining in. Toby nodded and made small conducting movements. When the chorus ended he craned round and said something to the bandit in the hide, then wriggled past Bill and went round to where Danny was standing under the window Mr Tolland had opened. (There was a cable going up through it now, with a telephone our end. I hadn't seen it fixed because I'd been helping with supper.) Toby explained something. Danny, looking bored and flat now, nodded. Toby went across to the bottom step of the dais and held up his hands. The children stopped singing.

"Not so dusty, me dears," said Toby. "Do that on the night and we'll get by. Now, Bill's just dreamed up another twiddly bit—where's the second semi-chorus?"

Eight hands rose, scattered around the pews. I noticed Toby give a quick blink of surprise when he spotted one of them among the tribesmen—there weren't any of the real singers there, in theory—but then he nodded.

"Right-oh," he said. "Too much fuss to sit you all together. Now listen. First and second time round, just what you've been doing. Third time we'll split the second semi in half. You, Pansy, and Jane, and Tamar, and Beth, carry on as before. The other four—that's Veronica and Melly and the other Jane and Trish—you try this . . . What'll he do di di doo di di doo doo, dooooooo? Just for you four then—two and . . . Stop! That's an E now Melly—doooo . . . two and . . . Fine. Now let's put it

together. Ahab, verse three, My wife Jezebel . . . Oh, for
heaven's sake! We're rehearsing! It's a solo! You can all sing it
till you're sick when we've stopped, but just now, just this once,
do let poor old Ahab sing his solo solo. Right . . ."

Ahab sang, and the rest came in for the chorus. When they got
to the new bit I couldn't hear that it was worth it, and I certainly
didn't think you'd notice any difference once you'd got all the
smalls shrieking away, but Toby seemed pleased. He looked
across at Bill who stuck up a thumb.

"Spiffing!" said Toby. "Well, since we're here, let's do the
Jehu ride. I was going to have a special go at that anyway, after
the rehearsal. I'll give you the note. Daah. Three four and . . ."

Somebody was standing in the aisle beside me. I looked up
and saw it was a bandit—the one who'd told the ravens in the
vestry that he'd blow their legs off if they didn't say where Juan
was. He grinned at me and made a sign for me to shift along the
pew. Mrs Dunnitt made space by shoving her bundle of clothes
down onto the floor. She was a bit clumsy how she did it, and I
guessed that somewhere in the middle there might be a pair of
black wings and a black leotard. The bandit slipped in beside me.

"They sing pretty good," he said.

"Yes," I snapped.

It was an automatic reaction. I knew his tone exactly. We get
it from someone every year. For instance, *Prodigal Son* year Bill
asked a friend of his who runs a recording studio to tape the
music and two engineers turned up for the last dress rehearsal.
Afterwards we realised that they thought they'd been detailed to
record some potty little school play and they'd resented it.
They'd arrived a couple of hours late. They'd insulted everyone
in sight. They'd shifted Mr Tolland's lights when they were
getting their mikes up and then pretended they hadn't. They'd
trodden in some wet paint and left purple footsteps on Onward's
carpet. They'd expected everything to wait for them. But by the
time the rehearsal was over they'd realised they'd got egg on
their faces and started trying to make up for it by smarming

round saying things like this bandit had just said to me. And then, I remembered, they'd really sweated during the performances to get the tape as good as they could. That made me think perhaps it wouldn't do any harm if I acted a bit more friendly towards this bandit.

He was listening to the Jehu ride. This was one of Prue's specials. It came at the start of the last scene of all. In the Bible Ahab dies in a battle and Elijah gets taken up to heaven in a fiery chariot and several years pass, and then a general called Jehu organises a coup against the new king. He brings it off, but he's still got Jezebel to deal with, so he gets into his chariot and drives towards the palace. The Bible actually says you can tell it's him from a long way off because of the ferocious way he drives. Jezebel sees him coming, so she dolls herself up and when he reaches the courtyard she leans out of her window and mocks him, but Jehu calls to some slaves to throw her down and then he drives his chariot over her. That's when the dogs come and eat her to make the last of Elijah's prophecies come true.

Anyway Prue had persuaded Bill to write a whole extra piece in for the Jehu ride. The only words are "Drive, Jehu! Drive!" but it's amazing what Bill does with the music. The whole cast sing them except Jezebel and her handmaids who are waiting in the tower, and while they're singing they stream past Jehu, who's standing in his chariot lashing his horses on. He doesn't move, actually, but the crowd streaming past make him look as though he's forcing a path through a frenzied mob, all yelling him on "Drive, Jehu! Drive!" It starts pretty loud but it gets louder and louder and the orchestra blares away, great pell-mell chunks of Yahweh music . . . and then, sudden as switching off the radio, silence. The mob vanishes. Jehu stands in his chariot, alone in the courtyard of the palace. He looks up as Jezebel's voice drifts down from her tower, scorning his triumph, while one flute plays the Baal music, the last time you hear it. It's the sort of thing which is terrific if you get it right and a complete mess if you get it wrong.

Toby did a few bits and pieces, everybody singing quietly, then went back and started at the beginning of the Jehu ride. Some of the smalls had woken up—I expect they'd never managed to get to sleep, actually—and crept back into the pews to join in, but they didn't seem to have grasped that they were supposed to keep the volume down. It was difficult in any case —the music was so obviously meant to be belted out—and before long the older children were trying to keep their end up until the whole thing seemed to take off. Toby glanced across to where Danny was lolling against the south wall. Danny nodded, and after that Toby really whipped them into it. In a sort of way they were calling for Jehu to come and rescue *us*—I expect people in prisons often build up fantasies like that, a ritual or a magic that will somehow set them free—only of course it carries no weight in the real world where things are hard and solid, like cell walls, or the pews we sat on, or the pistol on which the bandit beside me was tapping out the beat of Bill's music.

The drive ended with its proper snap, and I thought that was it. But the flute lady—I didn't know her name—had hung onto her instrument and the Baal music piped up just behind me. Dinah, somewhere the other side of the centre aisle, floated the Jezebel solo through the hush. Nick Wintle—a big rough voice, never quite in true but he'd only got about three lines—bawled to the slaves to throw her down. Then there was supposed to be a really peachy bit of drumming to go with her slow-motion fall. Of course that was out, but some of the children managed a good enough imitation for Dinah to do her scream (which she'd been driving the neighbours nuts with, practising, for weeks). The children wanted to carry on imitating the music for the dance of the scavenger dogs, but Toby cut them short. The bandit beside me put his pistol in his lap and clapped enthusiastically.

"I wonder what they made of that out there," I said.

"Keep 'em guessing," he said. "Great noise, uh?"

"I wish you'd heard it with the orchestra."

"Maybe you'll put on the show for us tomorrow—just the kind of stuff Danny goes for."

"My name's Doll Jacobs," I said.

"Call me Chip."

He held out his hand, just like Ferdy used to. I shook it. There was a bit of a stir all round—adults shooing smalls back to bed, older children waiting to queue for the loo, Mrs Banks and Mrs Slim taking round trays of coffee—they'd got the big electric urn used for church fetes going. I should have been helping, but I thought I might do more good smarming up to this bloke Chip.

"Do you play anything?" I asked him.

"Guitar. Just a bit."

"I'd heard everyone in Matteo's a pretty hot guitarist, or thinks he is."

"Well, I guess so."

"Except the women?"

(This was all stuff I'd got from Juan when I'd made the mistake of saying in his hearing I thought Ferdy was pretty good on the guitar. He'd come out with the line about the women unasked, of course.)

Chip smiled and spread his hands in a sorry-but-that's-how-it-is gesture. With the handshake it made me realise how foreign he was, though I wouldn't have known to look at him—just a bony, beaky bloke, about twenty-three, brown eyes, hair darkish but not black.

"What's your kind of music?" I asked.

Amazingly it was almost the same as Adam's, very loud early seventies rock—we'd even been to the same Led Zeppelin concert last June. He'd been living in London since January, and before that he'd been in America for three years. When he was eighteen he was at university in Matteo and had got involved in a student uprising. Some of his friends had been killed and he'd been put in prison. I didn't ask if he'd been tortured—I know it sounds stupid, but I was embarrassed, almost as if I'd started asking him

personal questions about his sex life. But he told me the guards
had come for him one day wearing smarter uniforms than usual
so he guessed it was his turn to be shot, but instead they'd put
him and about twenty others on a truck and driven them to the
military airport and an American plane had flown them to the
States. Apparently Amnesty had been putting pressure on
enough governments for the thugs in Matteo to think it was
time they made a gesture. Also it was just after President Carter
had started in the USA, and he'd told President Blick he was
going to cut off aid unless Blick did something about his
political prisoners. In spite of this Chip was especially bitter
about the Americans. He said the fact that Carter had done that
showed that the Americans could have done something about
the Blick regime much sooner, and then the people who died
would still be alive. He was pretty disgusted about Mr Reagan's
election—he said things would be back where they were before
Carter. I asked him about Juan's uncle, Colonel Vanqui, who
was supposed to be going to take over when President Blick
died. Chip made a scornful gesture.

"I guess he'll turn out Blick Mark Two," he said. "Old
model, new trim. I'm surprised you've heard tell of him—you
British are usually so goddam ignorant about that kind of
thing."

"You ought to talk to Mrs Dunnitt," I told him. "She knows
a lot about Matteo. She's been on vigils outside the embassy and
so on."

"You don't say! She here?"

I was a bit nervous what she'd think, but she smiled her
dried-up smile when I introduced them. Chip leaned across to
shake hands, then decided to change places with me so that they
could talk. I listened for a bit but gave up because it was all about
people I'd never heard of. It seemed that Mrs Dunnitt had met
some of the older Mattean exiles, and knew a few of the ones
who were still in prison. I heard Chip telling her that somebody
had died in some place and saw her face go hard, so I guessed it

might be one of the torture prisons. But mostly it was the sort of gossipy chat two strangers get into when they find they've got a lot of friends in common—lovely for them but not much fun for anyone else. I switched off and leaned into the pew-corner.

This is going to be all right, I thought. I noticed that Toby had taken Prue over to talk to Danny, and I didn't think that was likely to be about politics or this siege. Danny'd actually said he was a drama teacher, hadn't he? The girl was supervising the loo-queue. I could only see her back, but she didn't seem to have softened much. She was standing on a pew, posed as ever, Indian-scout-watching-wagon-train now. The fourth bandit guarded us from the hide, older than the others, his face thin and tired but his gun ready. An unlit cigarette dangled from the corner of his mouth. I couldn't begin to guess what kind of a person he might be, but if two of the four were friendly so soon, that wasn't bad.

It was really pretty extraordinary, in fact. I'd have thought everyone knew that when you get into things like sieges the best thing for the hostages is if they can get their captors emotionally involved with them, so that's just the thing professional revolutionaries try to avoid. But of course Chip and his friends weren't professionals—they hadn't even had a chance to rehearse any of this—the last thing they'd expected was to get themselves stuck holding a churchload of children. What they'd rehearsed was snatching Juan and running off with him somewhere. Now they were probably just as shaken as we were, just as much longing for the odd friendly word.

That was fine, I thought. Let's keep it like that, and nobody'll get hurt. That was even more important, just because they were amateurs—God knows what they mightn't do if they were panicked. So the vital thing was to stay friendly, seem easy, keep the pressure down. Then everything would turn out all right. Why, we might even get the opera staged after all.

The telephone rang, very shrill, setting up echoes like an alarm bell. Everybody fell silent. Danny answered, listened, spoke only a couple of words and put the handset down, then looked across the pews till he spotted Chip and made a thumbs-up sign. Chip turn to me.

"Know the time?" he asked.

I showed him my watch. It was ten to ten. Lordie, I thought, only that! It felt like getting on for midnight.

"Your main BBC news is at ten o'clock on the radio?" Chip asked.

"That's right."

He didn't seem ready to move though, so I thought I might as well carry on with the good work.

"The girl who's with you . . ." I began.

"Angel," he said. (He didn't pronounce it the way I've written it, but with a short "A" and with the end somehow bitten off.)

"She doesn't look very South American," I said.

"She's the real thing," he said.

"Aren't you?"

"Not me. I'm half American for a start. My mother's from Texas. That's why I came out in the first batch Blick let go. I speak English before I speak Spanish. I'm not real Mattean. Sure, I'd like to be, but . . ."

"What about Danny?"

"I guess he's Mattean. But listen, he's a teacher. Al . . ." (he flicked his head towards the man in the hide) ". . . Al's a priest . . ."

"A priest!"

"Sure. Christianity of Liberation. He's better at speaking Latin than he is at English, you know? But us three, we're near pure European. And that means, in spite of ourselves, we're kind of colonialists still. Angel is different. She's part Indian, part African. Maybe a little Spanish, or even German, enough to make her real Mattean, but mostly native blood and slave blood, mixed. Danny and Al and me, maybe we're liberators. Angel's what we're liberating."

I nearly said she looked quite liberated enough to me, but he was so serious all of a sudden that I guessed he wouldn't have liked it, so I just did my best to look bright-eyed.

"Danny's boss," said Chip. "We let him know what we think, Al and me, but if he decides different we go along with him. So does Angel, but . . . well, if it's about something practical he doesn't pay much heed to her. But suppose it's something different, suppose, all this way from home, he wants to get a feel of Matteo, of what Matteo needs—you get me?—then he listens to Angel."

"I thought he was pretty good when he was explaining about Matteo earlier," I said.

"Sure. He's been on a high all day. Want to come and hear what your BBC's got to say about us?"

"Oh, yes, please."

Actually what I really longed for was a visit to the loo, but this seemed too good a chance to miss. I followed Chip up to the front of the stage. The police had sent in with the other things a super-looking radio which Danny had tucked into the bit of stage behind the pulpit—I don't know why—so that it couldn't be shot at from any of the windows, perhaps. He'd got it tuned and was fiddling with the volume. Kaleidoscope was still waffling on about the new Flash Gordon film. Danny glanced at me, then at Chip, then nodded.

"OK," he said. "Bring Mr Slim also."

I went and fetched him. As soon as we got back Chip, leaning against the edge of the stage, put his arm round my waist and drew me close to him. I didn't care for that at all, especially in front of all the opera—a lot of them at school with me, too, only a year or two behind. And Mum—she does her best but she's never been comfortable seeing any of her children cuddling up to anyone in public, even when it's a friend she thoroughly approves of, like Adam. You bastard, I thought. Only a few hours back you were holding a gun to my head to frighten a group of kids, and now this. And you know quite well I've got

to pretend to love it. Bastard. But then I thought I'd brought it
on myself, sort of, by being all smarmy and bright-eyed at him.
You can't win, once you start compromising.

The weather forecast said there would be yet more rain. The
pips peeped.

"The World Tonight," said the breathy, urgent voice.
"Douglas Stewart reporting. First the news headlines."

The news-reader began.

"A group of South American revolutionaries are holding a
hundred children and about twenty adults hostage in a West
London church. More about this in a moment. At the EEC
Heads of Government meeting . . ."

Blah blah blah. Get on with it. Everything was blah compared
to what was happening to us. I stopped minding about Chip's
arm—anything to be up here, listening to a voice from the real
sane world . . . The news-reader stopped. Douglas Stewart said
that after the news they would be talking to some kind of expert
about the political situation in Matteo and also to people actually
involved in the siege. The news-reader took over again.

"A group of revolutionaries from the South American
republic of Matteo have seized a church in the Kensington area
of London where a hundred children were rehearsing for a
concert. One man has been shot and is seriously ill in hospital.
For details over to David Tollemache in the radio car."

Now it was a man, his voice more urgent and jittery. I
wondered how close he was. Marvellous that Ferdy was still
alive. Sickening that they'd called the opera a concert. (I really
did feel that, even then. I was furious.)

"Tragedy struck this smart residential area of London," said
the man, "just as the children were gathering for a rehearsal of
their annual concert. Among them was the ten-year-old son of
the Mattean Ambassador in London. It is thought that the
revolutionaries had planned to kidnap the child on his way to
the church, but failed. According to eyewitnesses it was already
dark when the children crossed to the church from the houses

where they had been dressing up. The group containing the Ambassador's son were all in identical fancy-dress and accompanied by the boy's personal guard. As they were crossing the road a car drew up and three men, armed with automatic weapons, climbed out, but apparently the costumes and the darkness confused them long enough for the guard to draw his own gun and firing broke out. The guard fell, severely wounded, but meanwhile the children ran into the church, pursued by the three kidnappers. The police have no clear picture of what happened inside the church from that moment, but evidently the kidnappers failed to isolate the Ambassador's son before the alarm was raised and three police cars arrived on the scene. As they drew up shots were fired at them from the kidnappers' car and a fourth person, thought to be a woman, ran into the church.

"Over a hundred police have since arrived. Many of them are armed. The whole area has been sealed off. Mobile generators have been brought up and the church is now brilliantly illuminated from the outside—indeed from where I stand at the bottom of Dryden Avenue, which is as close as the police will permit the public to approach, it looks as though the building was illuminated for a major festival.

"There has been some communication with the kidnappers. Shortly after eight o'clock the main door of the church was opened and a man came out and talked for twelve minutes with Chief Superintendent Clinton, the police officer in charge of operations. The man is believed to have been one of the adults who was helping to organise the concert. While he talked a gun was pointed at him by a figure concealed behind the doors. At the same time a teen-age girl, also believed to be one of the concert assistants, stood in full view inside the doors with another gun trained on her.

"As a result of these conversations food and blankets have been sent in for the children, and a telephone link has been set up. In a statement twenty minutes ago Chief Superintendent

Clinton said that the kidnappers had made certain demands. He refused to go into details but it is believed that these are largely concerned with the release of political prisoners in Matteo, and with the publication in British media of a statement of the aims of the revolutionary group.

"Due to its proximity to the BBC Television Centre, the area is popular with theatre and TV personalities, many of whom have homes in these pleasant tree-lined streets and squares. Several of the hostages are children of well-known personalities, but the police have requested the media not to release any names or ask for interviews with the parents involved. It is however known that the conductor of the concert is Mr Toby Belaski, who has been responsible for a series of Early Music concerts on Radio Three. Along with the children there are some twenty adults in the church. All these, and all the children including the son of the Mattean Ambassador, are now thought to be in the hands of the kidnappers, but unharmed. Now back to Pauline Bushnell in the News Room."

I felt cold. Chip's arm had dropped from my waist, but I wasn't glad. I didn't dare look at anyone. I went numb while the news-reader read the stuff about the EEC and another row in the labour party and some soccer-hooligans being fined. Danny, Chip and Mr Slim were whispering together in Spanish. At last she ended and Douglas Stewart took over again. He'd got somebody from the Institute of Anglo-Hispanic Studies in the studio who explained in a dry, lecturing voice about Matteo and President Blick and the political prisoners and Amnesty and President Carter. It was just what Chip had told me, with different details. He even got in a bit about Colonel Vanqui being an anglophile and our government hoping to influence him to liberalise the regime when he took over, but I could sense that Danny and Chip were getting angrier and angrier. It wasn't what the man said, I realised—it was how he said it. They wanted trumpets and battle-cries and thundering speeches to match their own suffering and outrage, and the man was taking all their gestures from them and turning them stale and dingy. I remembered what I'd been thinking, only a few minutes before, about them being amateurs. This was another example. They'd been expecting far too much from this broadcast—almost the way children expect too much of some treat. Professionals would have known, they'd have been ready for the let-down. Suddenly the amateur bit didn't seem quite so cosy.

Next we listened to a tape of the statement by the policeman in charge, in which he managed to say less than I would have believed possible. Then, in spite of what he'd said before, the man in the radio car did an interview with one of the parents. He didn't tell us the name, but even before I heard the voice I knew who it would be. Mrs Drew is exactly like Veronica, only three times as old and six times as awful. She's an actress and specialises in frightful gushing mother-in-laws and social climbers and she doesn't have to act much to get them right. She sounded weepy and scared, but absolutely loving it. Then they went back to the studio for a telephone call to somebody from the Foreign Office who was also expert in saying not much, and back to the radio car for the man to say there were no further developments, and then the closing headlines, and that was it. Danny turned the radio off with a snap.

I felt awful. It was incredible how everything had changed, without anything being different in any way you could actually see. Half an hour before I had been smugging to myself about how cunning we were being at calming things down, and how it was all going to end quite soon in peace and happy-ever-after. And now we were right back in the nightmare. Danny, still in his ultra-calm voice, was getting at Mr Slim about something —I guessed it was not having his statement broadcast, as if Mr Slim could have done anything about that. Suddenly he swung to me.

"You lie," he purred. "He is still here, in this church."

"Who?" I managed to blurt. "Oh, Juan! I don't know! Honestly, I don't know! I thought . . ."

"It is on the BBC," he said, taking a step towards me. I tried to back off, but Chip grabbed me by the arm.

"They don't know either!" I gabbled. "They weren't sure. You heard them. 'Thought to be,' they said. And anyway they got it all wrong. They called it a concert, for God's sake! And fancy dress!"

I felt my voice wanting to begin to scream, but I took a hold on myself and stopped it in time and just stood there, panting. Mr Slim started turning what I'd said into Spanish but Danny cut him short. He stared at me. He turned and looked at the children for quite a long while, especially at the front pew on the north where Queenie and the rest of the ravens were sitting.

"OK," he whispered, not turning round. "We search this church. But first we parade all these children."

Chapter Nine

First we had to wake up all the smalls. A lot of them were awake already, wriggling and whining about how hard the floor was, but others were deep, deep in that first pit of sleep you drop into at the beginning of the night, and even when we hauled them out of their blankets and pushed them towards the pews they staggered and wandered and tried to crumple back onto the floor. I actually had to carry Jenny McWhirter to her place, and she fell fast asleep against Pandora Watts the moment I dumped her in the pew.

The bandits had ordered most of the adults to sit in the centre aisle, straight in front of the hide, with their hands clasped behind their heads. Then Mrs Banks and Mrs Slim and Mrs Dunnitt and I moved the children into a solid block on the front pews south of the centre aisle. When that was done the four of us had to go and sit with the other adults. Angel was in the hide. Her gun seemed to be breathing down my neck as I sat there.

The bandits told the children to pick their feet off the floor and put them on the shelf where the prayer-books are kept behind each pew, and then Chip went along peering under the pews. The first thing he spotted was Mrs Dunnitt's bundle of clothes. He gave a grunt of excitement—I suppose it might have looked like a small boy huddling there—but the child sitting above it pulled it out and showed him it was only blankets and things. I held my breath but the raven costume wasn't there. (I found out afterwards Mrs Dunnitt had managed to dump it among the wing-pieces the other ravens had taken off when we bedded them down.) After that I couldn't see what Chip was doing, but I could hear him working his way down the nave.

Searching the pews is nothing like as straightforward as it looks. I know, because I'd done it after every rehearsal—some idiot child always manages to leave an anorak or something. However systematic you are it's amazingly easy to miss something. Even with all the lights on the pews cast funny shadows, heavy enough to hide quite large objects, and also to make you think there's something there when there isn't. On his way back Chip discovered that the little back stage was hollow—in fact it's only a couple of stage boxes Mr Slim borrows from St Andrew's School every year, but there are steps fore and aft and the whole thing is lashed together, so there was a good deal of banging and grunting while Chip cut the ropes and heaved the pieces apart.

I hated that. I was pretty nervous, thinking of the parade of children Danny had talked about. I hadn't any idea what he'd do when he found Juan. I still couldn't believe he'd kill him, or even hurt him, but that didn't stop me being frightened—frightened not just for Juan but for all of us, because Danny was going to find out we'd been cheating him and then, instead of being neutrals as far as he was concerned—a herd of animals, almost, which he happened to have a use for—he'd think of us as enemies, vermin. My throat was dry and I kept swallowing, even before Chip started pulling the back stage to bits.

Nobody had told the children what was happening, or why, but they seemed to have guessed—the way they do—that it was really serious now. They sat absolutely still. In fact the whole church was dead silent except for the noises Chip made. Every bang and boom set up dull, hateful echoes until I felt like an animal in a hole, a badger men are digging out in order to kill while it cowers into its furthest tunnel and listens to the thud and grate of the spades. Chip was digging in the wrong place at the moment, but he'd come to his victim in the end.

When Chip was sure Juan wasn't hiding anywhere in the nave,

Danny made Mr Tolland go and turn on the Elijah spot again.
Then he called me and Mrs Dunnitt out—we were at the front
of the adults squatting in the aisle because we'd gone in last.
Chip gave us our orders.

"Now see here," he said. "This better be done right. We're
going to look at every goddam kid, one at a time, under the
spotlight. As soon as we're through with each kid they got to
come over this other side and sit close up on the benches. If there
are twelve kids on one bench that side, I want to see the same
twelve kids on the same bench this side. OK? So you, Mrs, you
go and tell them when to come out from the benches, and Doll,
you pack them back in this side. When you finish one bench,
you stop, and I'll check you've got the right number and then I'll
count the kids on the next bench and you don't go on till I've
done that. Right?"

He had a photograph in his hand while he was talking. He
didn't show it to us, but I caught a glimpse when he turned to
check whether Danny was ready to start. It was a snapshot of
Juan, standing against a background of gaudy colour—beach-
brollies, I think. I only saw it a moment but I knew that look
exactly, proud as a prince, male as a tom-cat, staring con-
temptuously at the camera, only one small boy on a beach but in
his own mind the President of his country, with his palace guard
goose-stepping past on his birthday parade and his air force jets
screaming in close formation overhead.

Chip took the photo to Danny and then went and counted the
children in the far front pew, making a real business of it. Angel
was still on duty in the hide, but at least Danny'd allowed the
adults sitting in the aisle to put their arms down. I saw Mum
gazing out at nothing with a strange, dreamy look and I realised
I hadn't even spoken to her since the bandits had burst in. When
he was ready Chip signalled to Mrs Dunnitt, who beckoned
Camilla Richardson to go and stand under the spotlight.
Camilla's one of the older ones—fourteen—but she could
hardly move, she was so frightened. When she was in the full

glare of the light Danny stopped her and put his hand over her beard—she was Chief Courtier—then checked with the photograph and told her to come over to me. Mrs Dunnitt sent the next child—it was Inigo Farquson-Colquhoun—up onto the stage.

Danny took longer to decide that Inigo wasn't the one he was looking for. From where I stood the brightness of the spot made the far side of the nave, with only the ordinary church lights on, seem half-dark, but I noticed Mrs Dunnitt absent-mindedly adjusting the next child's costume as if this were part of just another rehearsal. By now all the children were wide awake again. They knew what was happening—what was going to happen. I was certain that all their mouths were dry with fright, like mine, and all their hearts uselessly hammering as they waited for the moment. The awful thing was not to be able to stop hoping at the same time as you knew we hadn't a hope. As I packed the children into the pew I whispered to each of them "Don't stare," until I noticed Angel was watching me with a still gaze, like a cat stalking a bird.

When that pew was full Chip came and counted the children, and then counted the next row on Mrs Dunnitt's side before he let her start sending them up, and he made sure everyone could see what he was doing. By then I could hardly think. Juan was in the third pew.

For rehearsals the children sit in groups—tribesmen, Baal-priests or whatever—because it helps them sing together, but the bandits had herded them in all hugger mugger. Even so four of the handmaids had managed to stick with each other. It's a bit of a tradition in the opera that the wicked women tend to be cronies and go about in a gossipy gang, but I guessed they'd made a special point of it in order to help hide Juan. I could see his green and silver costume third from the end. By the time it was their turn I was sure that the bandits must actually know now that they were getting warm. We were all so taut, so breathless with tension, that I could even hear a tiny trickle of falling water as though somebody had left the kitchen tap on.

Philippa Wimbush was first. She slunk out of the pew with her veil half across her face but Mrs Dunnitt snatched it clear and stroked it back over her shoulders. While she stood like a whipped puppy in front of Danny I heard the tinkling water-noise more clearly. It seemed to be coming from a different place, but before I could worry about it I had to get Philippa into her pew. Next came Emma Banks. Thinking about it now I could almost laugh, she looked so like her mother. No doubt she was just as scared as Philippa, but in her it came out as fury. She stood in front of Danny in her violet gauze with her head held stiff and sideways—just like Mrs Banks in one of her rages—determined not even to glance at him, and when he flicked his hand for her to come down to me she paid no attention for at least a couple of seconds and then stalked away.

While I was slotting Emma into place I noticed that something was wrong among the children in the two front pews—they were fidgeting and looking at each other—but I hadn't time to think about it. In spite of what I'd said to the others I simply had to watch had happened to Juan. I saw Mrs Dunnitt twitch and pluck at his costume, just the way she'd done with most of the others. I don't think she said anything to him. My heart tried to stop beating as he glided into the spotlight, and I almost gasped aloud. It was the first time I'd dared to look at him direct. I remembered Mrs Dunnitt had been up by the front vestry door when the bandits had burst in and Veronica had been there too. She'd probably hustled Juan and Veronica into the vestry, which was why so many of the children knew what she'd done. Even so, she could hardly have had more than a couple of minutes, so the difference was amazing. She'd smeared his lips luscious red and made a pink blob on each cheek and shadowed his eyes bright blue, so that he looked like a wicked doll. I'd never realised what marvellous eyes he had, blue and clear, with great long lashes. He stopped at the dead centre of the spot and stared straight at Danny, looking utterly contemptuous. One shoulder twitched up a little. I've no idea whether he did it on purpose but I'm sure I've seen exactly that shoulder twitch before. It was a late-night movie, the sort where they show antique Hollywood B films. There was this bitchy blonde getting out of her Cadillac outside some super-posh restaurant when the down-and-out-hero came up and spoke to her—he'd been in love with her since their schooldays, or saved her life or something like that—and she twitched up her shoulder and turned away through the restaurant doors without one word. Of course it wouldn't have worked without Mrs Dunnitt's costume, which was far, far sexier than acres of naked flesh could possibly have been, but even so . . .

There was a louder trickle of water, almost a gush, quite close, and a muttering among the children. Danny glanced up and at the same moment I realised what had been happening. Some poor kid, in the tension and strangeness, had wet her pants, and that had set others off. I even thought I could smell the faint reek of pee. Chip looked across at Danny with a shrug. Danny smiled. Next I knew Juan was gliding down the steps and edging along the third pew to sit beside Emma Banks. Danny didn't even seem to have noticed him go.

I finished my part of the parade in a sort of daze. Three words ran through and through my mind—one of Adam's favourite cliches—*People aren't things*. I suppose I was telling myself that however clever you are, however much power you have even if you've got a loaded gun in your hand to point at people, you still can't be sure what's going to happen. In a way Danny had beaten himself. He'd screwed us up to that pitch of fright on purpose. He could easily have arranged the parade to take place out of sight. He didn't need the spotlight. But he'd gone for the drama of it—I remembered he used to be a drama teacher—and by doing things that way he'd caused something to happen which he hadn't bargained for, and it had distracted him just enough to make him miss Juan. Nothing that any of us could have done on purpose—coughed, or had hysterics or thrown a fit or something—would have worked, because he'd have guessed. But half a dozen kids wetting their pants in a nightmare —it was so *natural*. It was comic. It changed things, so that when the rest of the children came and stood under the spotlight, though they didn't seem anything like as scared as the first two pews had been, that looked natural too.

Luckily most of them were still fairly scared, or sleepy, or shy—especially the ones who'd wet themselves—but a few were stupid enough to look smug and sly, and Veronica Drew positively attempted to flirt. I could sense Danny becoming tense with frustration—I was beginning to realise that his calmness was only a mask—and I started to worry again. All we'd done was get through one bad moment, and now there were hours and hours still to go—even days and days—and there'd be plenty more bad moments and even the times between were going to be awful enough.

When the last child had paraded Danny stood in the spotlight.

"Now listen to this, you kids," he said. "You want to go home, I think. You want all to sleep in your own bed, yes?"

They muttered, looked at each other and back at him, rows of pale faces smeared with make-up and shadowy-eyed with tiredness, hoping but not trusting. I guessed they'd changed their minds about Danny. They didn't like him any more.

"OK," he said. "Soon you go home. But first all you must do is one thing. You tell me where is hiding Juan O'Grady. I give my sacred promise we do not hurt him, not one hair. OK? Now you say where he is, and when we see him you all go home."

He waited. They froze, mistrusting each other as much as him, waiting for a lead. After all, Juan hadn't made himself particularly popular.

"Honestly we haven't a clue," said a voice. I recognised it as Tristan Pierce.

They murmured agreement. They began to say the words aloud. In a moment they'd be shouting. Danny held up his hands and got them quiet.

"OK, you don't tell me," he said. "So nobody go home. Everybody must sleep on this hard floor. You are the choosers of this, you know. Take away this light, please."

He walked off the stage.

All this had taken much longer than you'd think, and on top of that the bandits had tougher ideas about sleeping arrangements now. They couldn't make us all sleep in places where we could be shot at from the hide, but they packed about thirty into the centre aisle and along the dais below the stage. They mixed children—even quite small ones—in with the adults, but I managed to make sure I got myself a space next to Mum, right at the front of the aisle. Everybody else slept on pews. By the time all this was arranged it was getting on for midnight and Danny and Chip went off to listen to the last radio news on BBC4. I wrapped my blanket round me and lay down next to Mum.

"Are you all right?" I whispered.

"Don't worry, darling, it isn't true," she murmured in a far-away voice. That was what she used to say, ages ago, when I had my nightmare about the balloons and she would come up and walk around the room with me in her arms, holding me tight until the shuddering stopped. It wasn't much comfort now. I wondered if she even realised what she was saying.

I'd hardly decided on a posture which wouldn't be agony when Chip came and prodded me with his foot. Achingly I wriggled out of the blankets.

"How did it go?" I whispered.

"Get the Slim fellow," he answered.

Searching the church for Juan took absolute ages. Even at the start I could hardly think what I was doing, I was so tired. I expect the bandits thought it would be quite simple—there doesn't seem anywhere much to search, just the nave and choir, three or four rooms and a few nooks and crannies. But once you start there seem to be endless odd corners in which a child could

hide, and what's worse most of them are appallingly lit. The
back gallery for instance, hasn't only got the organ in it. There's
a great empty space beyond where the choir used to sit in
Victorian times but it's had all its seats taken out and for seventy
years people have been putting things there which they can't
think what else to do with, and there was only one dirty yellow
light shining on piles of dusty church gunge and bits of stage
from earlier operas and left-overs from Michaelmas Fetes and so
on, not to mention Mr Tolland's lighting cables snaking all over
the place because that's where he controls things from. And then
there was the actual organ, which looks huge but isn't solid all
through. Nobody's allowed to touch it except Miss Mendlicott,
the organist, because it's very delicate and temperamental and
expensive to mend; it often goes haywire in the autumn because
of the change in temperature and then the anti-opera people in
the Church Council say some of us must have got up into the
gallery and fiddled around with it, though we've got a strict rule
that no one except Mr Tolland and Mr Slim is allowed up there.
Anyway now Mr Slim had to fiddle with a vengeance, finding
out how to take off all sorts of side-panels and using Mr
Tolland's torch to let Danny peer in among the pipes and tubes
—like looking in a bramble-thicket for a baby rabbit Noggin has
caught at the cottage and brought into the garden to tease and as
soon as you've got him to drop it it's limped away and you feel
you've got to make sure it's not too wounded but now it's
cowering in the bramble and you can't even see the stupid
creature . . . I don't think, even when we'd finished with the
organ, Danny can have really been sure he hadn't missed Juan,
cringeing somewhere among the dusty shadows. *We* knew, of
course, but we couldn't say. It was incredibly frustrating,
having to go on when you ached to curl up and sleep, and trying
not to let them see you were sure it was no use because you
actually knew where Juan was hiding.

Danny and Chip got frustrated too. They started to argue
with each other in Spanish, because Chip insisted on making a

thorough job of the search while Danny became more and more casual about it. He seemed actually bored, not just with searching but with the whole siege business, as though it was a game he'd started and now wanted to get out of. Luckily I'd found the ring of spare keys in the sacristy so we didn't have to bust anything open. I was even able to show them that the wardrobe in the choir-vestry had nothing in it except surplices. Danny got excited again when I showed them the "secret" passage under the High Altar, but Mr Slim found a spare light-bulb and put it in a socket I didn't know was down there so they could see no one was hiding in the general mess. When we came out into the sacristy another argument began, quite loud, until Danny suddenly lost patience and strode away. Chip shrugged and blew a long breath through his mouth. We three went on with the search alone.

Next time we passed through the nave I saw that Danny had made himself some kind of bed by the telephone and was lying on his back, wide awake, staring up at the rafters. All my friends were laid out in hummocky rows like dead bodies after a plane disaster, and the bandit called Al—the one who'd been a priest —was perched at the back of the hide, motionless, with his gun held sideways across his chest, ready to swing it out and blaze away if the people outside tried any tricks. I was glad it wasn't the girl. I'd seen her lying in front of the High Altar, curled up on a mound of old altar-hangings she'd dragged out of the chest in the front vestry. Chip had picked up the radio and tuned it to LBC, so we finished the search to the sound of insomniacs phoning in from places like Pinner and Walthamstow with grouses about anything from race relations to street lighting. They always sound as though they all have cleft palates. That night there was a dear old thing who couldn't get the police to take an interest in the fact that the Russians were deliberately putting out poisoned food for her cat. There were news headlines every quarter of an hour. They always started with us but they didn't say anything new.

Somewhere around half past two even Chip was satisfied, and I staggered off and lay down. Mum was wide awake. She didn't say anything but reached for my hand and gripped it tight. It was her left hand. Its muscles are incredibly strong from all those years of fingering the big cello strings, and though she didn't actually hurt it felt as though she wasn't ever going to let me go. And in spite of my tiredness the floor felt like concrete.

Chapter Ten

It wasn't really a dream—I was mostly too restless for proper dreams—but I kept having an imaginary conversation with Mrs Dunnitt, the sort of almost-dream argument that runs through and through your mind when you're worried or ill and can't sleep. I expect it was the hardness of the floor that set me off—though I had a kneeler for a pillow and a layer of carpet and a couple of folds of blanket beneath me, so it wasn't really like lying on bare rock. But I kept remembering what she'd said about people living in caves and the privileged ones being allowed to sleep near the fire while the others huddled against the wall. And then I'd actually drop off for a bit and dream I was in the cave, or else in a bare hut in the desert with guards outside, and prowling Alsatians, and electrified fences. Then I'd wake up and remember there really were people living like that, years on end, so though I was having a bad night I was still one of the lucky ones.

We even had the church heating on, which was a mercy or we'd all have frozen. The noise of the fans roared in and out of my dreams. And of course the bandits kept the lights full on, and I've never been any good at sleeping except in the proper dark. The children were pretty restless—there was usually a bit of quiet crying going on somewhere, and fidgets and mutters of complaint when somebody turned or threshed and disturbed a neighbour, and comings and goings to the loo, and fits of coughing.

But I did doze, off and on, whereas I don't think Mum slept all night. Whenever I was awake enough to know where I was she was lying beside me, still as a log with her eyes shut but her specs still on and a look of total concentration on her face. I knew she was playing scores in her head, and if I hadn't been so knackered I'd have worried more. She does that a bit sometimes, on bad days, but not usually for hours on end, all the music she knows, bar by bar from beginning to end to fill her mind up and stop her thinking about anything else. That's a bad sign. Just before she had her breakdown she did it a lot, Trog told me—I was too small to notice, of course. If only we'd been on better terms with the bandits—like we were before they heard the ten o'clock news—I could have asked if I could send round for Mum's Valium. I really wanted to do something for her. She'd let go of my hand at some point, but when I tried to take hers again she pushed mine away.

I did have one proper dream, just before I woke up. It wasn't like any of the others. It began as part of the opera. In the story, after the raven bit, Elijah goes and hides from Jezebel's soldiers in a country to the north. He's staying with a woman when her son dies, but Elijah takes the boy up to his own room and somehow brings him back to life and carries him back down to his mother. In my dream I saw this happening—just Elijah coming down the ladder with the boy in his arms. I think I was the mother, and though I should have felt overjoyed I wasn't because I knew something ghastly was going to happen, and then I saw the boy was Juan O'Grady.

I don't think Elijah was actually Danny in my dream. I think that must have been something I invented, sorting the dream out to make sense of it while I was coming awake, but as soon as I was really awake and thinking about it I saw how the pattern fitted in other places. Danny was Elijah. Senora O'Grady could be Jezebel. President Carter would do for Ahab—of course he wasn't really married to Juan's mother, but you could argue that the USA is sort of married to all those South American countries in an uncomfortable kind of way. And Danny's friends in the camps were the murdered prophets . . . Or perhaps it was us, the rich and cosy people trying to do our best provided it didn't mean losing our money or our sleep, who ought to be Ahab . . . I began to have a different idea.

There was one moment in the opera the children particularly hated, and kept asking the mafia if they couldn't get Bill to make something different happen. It wasn't any of the obvious things which had worried the mafia in the first place—Jezebel being flung screaming from her tower and being scrunched by Jehu's chariot wheels, or the Baal-priests getting torn to bits by the mob, or anything like that. It was the sacrifice of the bulls. The other horrors were somehow normal, the sort of thing you get on TV or in story-books. But the idea of having a religion in which you took a harmless animal and chopped it up on an altar to please your God—yuck, they thought, and I suppose I did too. I mean I can imagine what it's like to want to take some pretty horrible revenges on your tribal enemies, but I can't imagine what it's like to believe that slaughtering bulls and pouring the blood about will make God happy.

Now, lying on that ghastly floor, the thought came into my head that our part in the pattern was to be those bulls. I remembered what Bill had said. Spouting blood. Blood Everywhere. Terriblydramatic . . . A sacrifice . . . A gesture . . . Something that Bill had only mumbled shot into my mind, about the Temple courtyard being inches deep in blood with all the animals being sacrificed at Passover. There will be no blood. Mrs Dunnit had said that. But now, clear as a photo in a colour supplement I saw this church, our church, quite empty, but with the whole floor rippling red. Onward's new carpet.

I sat bolt upright, trying to jerk the picture out of my mind. Chip was guarding us in the hide now. He raised an eyebrow at me and I made signals that I wanted to go to the loo. He nodded and I picked my way out.

There was still only the one church loo, though the people outside had promised us a couple of portable ones, according to

Mr Slim. The bandits couldn't spare one of themselves to do loo-guard all the time, so you had to queue in the cross-aisle till they were ready. Then they unbolted the kitchen door, scouted very cautiously in and made sure there weren't any paratroopers lurking around. Then one of them stood guard in the kitchen and let us in one at a time.

When I got there the kitchen door was bolted. The only other person in the queue was little Imogen Fitzroy, hopping from foot to foot and looking anxious. It was twenty past six according to my watch. While I waited, doing my best not to hop too, I noticed lying in the first of the pews my own opera file—an old yellow one I'd bought for physics notes when I was doing O-level, all doodled over on the outside with my usual pattern of daisy-heads, mixed in with things like phone numbers and times of concerts and addresses for parties. For something to do I picked it up and began to leaf through. Another couple of children joined the queue behind me. At last Chip and the girl, Angel, turned up and did their anti-paratroop drill and Chip came out, leaving her to see us through. I passed him on my way back.

"Hi, Doll," he said. "Sleep well?"

"No," I said. "But look . . ."

I showed him the page where I'd written my very first cast-list, under the piano in Mrs Banks's drawing-room. Of course I'd copied it out several times since then for other people, but it had never seemed worth the trouble of making an extra one just for my own file when I knew it all by heart anyway. It was smothered with scribblings and arrows and crossings-out, but it still made sense to me.

"There *are* only six ravens, you see," I said.

He turned the page. That was all right, because I'd used the back of the next sheet—the one with only Juan's name on it— to write out a notice to pin on the church door a couple of weeks before. He turned back.

"Spend all night getting this written?" he said.

"I spent all night searching the bloody church," I said.

"OK, OK. Better get back to your place."

"You don't think it's . . ."

"Sure. They're saying the same on the radio now. The kid's believed to be at the embassy."

"Then . . ."

"There's some pretty sophisticated bugs around, Doll. Remember that spat Danny and me had in that office place last night? Your friends outside would have listening devices planted all round—they'd have picked that up, or something else someone said, and fed the newsmen this stuff about the kid being at the embassy, uh?"

"Yes, but . . ."

"I'll tell Danny," he said, handing my file back to me. "Go and lie down now."

I lay on my back and waited for morning. It was rather like the end of one of those nights when you're starting flu or measles or something, and you feel pretty ghastly but there's no hope of going to sleep again and you seem to lie and wait for ever before somebody comes in and pulls your curtains and asks if you want any breakfast. I really didn't feel too good—sick and sore and stiff and cold and mucky-mouthed, with a vile dull headache. I expect most of the others felt the same. A lot of them were stirring now, taking the chance to go to the loo or simply easing their aches by sitting up and leaning back to back with a friend. We still looked like people after a disaster, but at least live ones, not dead. Danny himself was in the hide with one of the automatic weapons, but he paid very little attention to what we were up to. For quite long periods he actually had his eyes shut, not asleep but brooding.

A few of the smalls when they woke up began by kneeling with their hands together in front of their mouths and their eyes closed, saying their prayers. Provided they had their backs to you they looked perfectly sweet, but their faces were all smeared with tears and make-up, and had that bruised look round the eyes you get from a bad night's sleep, which rather spoilt the Christmas card effect. A gang from the Godolphin Upper Fifth had been into meditation that term, and were sitting cross-legged in the lotus posture, doing their thing. Jezebel's hand-maids were in their usual huddle. Somehow they'd got hold of Mrs Dunnitt's kit and were repairing each other's make-up as though it was the most natural thing in the world. The one in green and silver was still lying flat and the others were making a bit too much of a show of treating their companion as a slug-a-bed while they worked on her. I saw a lazy arm stretch out in languor. Just Juan's thing, I thought sourly, dossing down among the beauties. Lucky for everyone he wasn't a few years older and the lights were on all night! It struck me suddenly that it was Juan who'd ruined the whole opera. But for him, at this moment I'd be waking up in my own bed and beginning to think about the dress rehearsal and whether it had been a wow or a disaster or in between and how I was going to get the shoe-drill right to-night. Bloody Juan. Even in the handmaids' whispers I could hear an undertone, as if they'd been the chorus in a quite different kind of opera, the idiot sort where the two gentlemen have to dress up as women and get into the harem to rescue their ladies or something—twee, pretty-pretty and oh-so-smirky about sex. Dad had taken us down to Glyndebourne for my fifteenth birthday treat to see one of those, and I'd loathed it all except the music. Serve the little tarts right, I thought now, if they drew enough attention to themselves to get Juan spotted after all.

"Sleep all right, darling?" whispered Mum.

"So-so. What about you?"

"Like a log," she lied.

I reached out my hand. She squeezed it gently and put it aside.

"I wanted to make some fresh yoghurt this morning," she said in a dreamy voice.

"It's not the end of the world," I whispered.

"Oh. No. I suppose not."

People often say that cellists are the bossiest of the string-players. It comes of having to keep the bass-line steady while the violins and violas go tweedling around above. Mum does have a bit of that in her—after all it was Mum who really got the opera going in the first place, all those years ago—but just from what she said about the yoghurt I decided that she'd somehow come to the conclusion that this siege business wasn't anything to do with her. It was a nuisance—a bit like a strike of electricians at some hall where she was supposed to be playing and there was nothing for the orchestra to do except sit around and swap musical gossip while someone else sorted the mess out. With certain kinds of unpleasantness—they don't have to be anything to do with music—she takes that line. I was relieved, as much as anything. I didn't want to have to try and get her Valium sent in, partly because it would mean bothering the bandits with one more thing—and though Chip seemed pally again this morning I couldn't be sure about the others—but mainly because Mum regards her tranquillisers as a really private thing, and would hate the idea of anyone outside the family knowing anything about them.

A long time later—you couldn't tell whether it was dark still outside because of the floodlights on the tall windows, but I vaguely felt that their glare was changing as real light seeped into the sky—a long time later Chip came and fetched me. I could see he was pretty tired, but he looked quite friendly in an edgy kind of way.

"Danny wants to see your book," he said.

"Anything fresh on the radio?"

"Still saying the kid's at the embassy."

"They're learning. They'll realise it's an opera, next, and stop calling it a concert."

When we reached the hide Danny handed his gun to Chip and began to leaf listlessly to and fro through my file. He took ages. He looked at pages that really couldn't have interested him at all, like lists of old rehearsal schedules. I began to get a bit panicky about whether there wasn't something to do with Juan somewhere else in the file . . . The embassy phone number! I'd have to say that was mainly for Ferdy . . .

"Did the radio say anything about the guard?" I whispered to Chip.

"Still alive," he said without turning from watching his hostages, alert in spite of his weariness.

"Still critical?" I asked.

"Uh huh. Matter so much?"

"Some of the children are very fond of him. It's important to keep them happy. I mean, they're going to get pretty restless today."

"Now see here, Doll, honey. Kids are tough. I've seen it, places far worse than this, and far longer. This can't go on more than three more days, outside. I've seen kids put up with it months . . . years. No medicine. One meal a day, one small bowl of corn. Don't you try to wring my heart with the idea that these fat little porkers are suffering. All they're getting is a bit of schooling. Everyday life in the Third World, uh?"

"Still, you can't *want* them restless . . ."

"OK we give them something to do," broke in Danny's purring voice. "Perhaps you play this play for us. I think it is very interesting."

"Well . . ." I began.

"Chip is right. We have some schooling. Yes."

"Anyway you'll have to ask the mafia," I said.

"Huh?" grunted Chip.

"The mafia?" said Danny, even more slowly than usual.

"Oh, I'm sorry," I said. "It's what we call the people who run the opera—Mrs Banks and my mother and the Slims and Mrs Dunnitt are the main ones."

It was the first time I'd seen Danny really smile, apart from the charisma-faces he'd made when he was talking to the children. It gave me a pang, it was so like Ferdy's smile.

"Is everywhere, the mafia," he said. "You have also the CIA?"

"Not as far as I know," I said.

"Then you have the CIA. Is now time Chip sleeps. I stay guard. When Al comes you find Mr Slim. He use the telephone and make arrangement for food to come."

Everything took simply ages. Getting the breakfast in, for instance, meant almost an hour of hanging around with the food getting colder and colder on the pavement outside and us getting hungrier and hungrier a few yards away inside until Al was absolutely sure that the system was secure and that none of the people outside even thought they might have a chance of trying something clever. I got blasé about standing in the porch with a gun pointing at me—except when it was Angel pointing the gun. You couldn't get blasé about her. Outside I could see a shiny soft morning, warm for December, with a few puffy clouds in a pale blue sky beyond the bare branches of the Dryden Avenue planes. The Avenue was almost empty—just like a summer Sunday when everyone's off for the weekend and there's hardly a car parked against either pavement. But there was a solid crowd beyond the Kingswood Road crossing, held back by some sort of barrier. Above the crowd I could see the roofs of vans with TV cameras set up on them, all pointing straight at me. They'd have zoom lenses, too. I was terribly tempted to wave to Granny Jacobs—I knew she'd be watching, eyes glued to the telly, ear glued to the phone, gabbing to some crony about how horrible it all was. Granny Tope would be watching too, bolt upright, alone, appalled by the publicity as much as the thing itself. I yearned even for her. When at last they shut the big red doors and we went back into the nave it looked and smelt and felt grimy, stale, hopeless.

We got the portable loos in at another session and they were an absolute mercy. We put them in the back vestry and declared it to be the Ladies. A lot of clothes came in at the same time, collected from the changing-houses, but by then the rumour had somehow got round that there was going to be a rehearsal, so most of the children only half-changed, putting on jeans under their robes and cardigans and jerseys over. At least this meant that the handmaids could carry on camouflaging Juan by all staying as feminine as possible, but they'd probably have done that anyway, knowing them. I'd got a message through about extra pants and jeans for all the smalls who'd had bad luck, too.

None of the bandits came to the mafia session when we argued about whether to do the rehearsal or not. There was a bit of hassle because Mrs Banks took the line that we should refuse, simply because it was what the bandits wanted, or at least insist on getting something in exchange. The Slims said it would keep the children happy for a bit and help lower the tension. Toby said the orchestra were all in favour. Mum hardly said anything, and nor did Mrs Dunnitt—in fact Mrs Dunnitt positively refused to express an opinion. I trotted to and fro between the mafia and Danny, checking whether he'd let Mr Tolland go up into the gallery to do the lights and so on. He said yes to everything. He seemed utterly bored and listless, just like a child refusing to play some game because it isn't the one he wanted. When Angel took over from him in the hide he went and lay on a pile of hangings by the telephone, but when it rang he wouldn't answer it, though it went on for minutes on end. He wouldn't even take it off the hook. The noise really got on your nerves. It made the church feel like a vast hollow tooth, with toothache.

So although things seemed to get better all morning—break-fast, dry pants, warm clothes, extra loos, the rehearsal to look forward to—somehow they felt as if they were getting worse. It was mostly that beastly telephone, and having Angel in the hide doing her rattlesnake trick, and Danny's listlessness. And we were all so tired and stale, too—the children, the orchestra, the mafia, the bandits, everyone. I began to long for the rehearsal, just so that something different could happen.

We didn't start till after lunch (some crazy mum must have baked a load of home-made whole-meal, and we tried to cheer each other up with jokes about the honour of being in the world's first health-food siege). The rehearsal was pretty dreadful, honestly. Nobody's heart was in it, I suppose, though by then the children had stopped being scared stiff—in fact they seemed to have got much more used to the siege business than the adults. They didn't seem to realise that just because they hadn't been hurt yet it didn't mean they might not be, any moment. But they were all dead tired, and there wasn't much of an audience, except for Chip in the hide, and Danny lolling up on his elbow to watch from his bedding, and Angel perched on the back of a pew behind us. I turned round now and then and saw her staring at the stage with intense, unreadable eyes. Despite her super-chic get-up I began to see what Chip had meant about her being a peasant. She might have been the witch of a jungle tribe, even. I almost persuaded myself that the rehearsal was going so badly because she was putting a spell on it, but of course it was only that we were all so tired and the only magic was the daylight streaming in through the church windows, casting a spell of ordinariness stronger than any wizardry Mr Tolland could work with his lights.

It was all a bit like one of those films of nutty inventors trying to fly by muscle-power, with Toby sweating away to get the opera airborne while it trundled and trundled along the runway. Once or twice it gave a little hop and I thought it was going to take off at last, but then it flopped back. Almost from the start the children got things wrong, and after a while Toby gave up and let them just go through the motions.

The only good thing about this was that it wasn't so obvious, when Juan came on with the handmaids, that he hadn't much clue what he was supposed to be up to. Because of Bill's system of rehearsing things separately and fitting them together later he'd probably only seen the handmaids rehearsing a couple of times, and being Juan he wouldn't have felt all that interested.

All he could do was follow Philippa Pomeroy round the stage and copy her movements while the others sang, but he got through the first court scene all right. I felt myself relax as the mass of children melted away for the scenes with Elijah in exile—first the ravens, then bringing the widow's son back to life. The raven scene was a real mess. It was extraordinary how much it mattered, missing the seventh bird.

Then came Mount Carmel, and all at once the opera gave one of those hops I was talking about, as though it was going to take off and fly after all. The Baal-priests really got going on their dance, and Jake was haggard with tiredness and his voice came out all rough, which suited Elijah as he mocked their efforts, and the Baal shout and the Yahweh shout clashed and shrieked and the orchestra weighed in fortissimo and all at once you got a glimpse of what the whole thing might be about. I glanced round to see how Angel was taking it, but she'd got off her pew and was talking with Chip in the hide, arguing about something. As soon as she went back to her place we were down on the ground again, trundling.

That was the bit about the whirlwind and the fire and the still small voice which privately all the mafia had wanted Bill to cut because even on good days the wheedling, scritchy music he'd written didn't seem to do much except hold the story up. Then came the Naboth's Vineyard bit. (Ahab wants to buy the vineyard to add to his garden. Naboth won't sell. Jezebel has him framed for blasphemy and stoned to death which means that Ahab can legally confiscate the vineyard, but he doesn't enjoy it for long because Elijah turns up out of nowhere and tells him that the dogs will lick his blood in the place where he's standing and what's more Jezebel's going to get eaten by dogs too.)

This had been the children's favourite bit from the moment they first heard it. Usually they go for the loud, bouncy tunes, but Bill had written an absolutely dreamy song for the hand-maids to sing. There was no special scenery—we don't do things that way—just a couple of slaves holding token vines while the handmaidens drifted about singing how lovely the garden is, and the tune had simply caught on, like a pop song. I'd even heard kids at school who'd nothing to do with the opera singing it. It was funny, because secretly Mum and the really musical people slightly despised the garden song for being too pretty, but they couldn't get out of the fact that it really had something which a lot of posh clever music hasn't got.

This was another of the places where the rehearsal almost took off, despite Juan usually being in the wrong place. Veronica must have sung her own lines—it's the sort of music it's difficult to tell where it's coming from, and anyway half the children couldn't help joining in where they sat. The one thing that didn't work at all was the lighting, because of the daylight streaming through the windows. Mr Tolland had arranged a sort of drifting green-and-yellow dappled effect, like the shadow under summer trees, with darkness beyond. Then, in the middle of the darkness, Elijah is suddenly there, come out of nowhere, standing in a hot orange spot. Ahab goes ashy (Mr Tolland playing with his lights like an organist) and sings "Have you found me, O my enemy?" and Elijah bawls his prophecy and vanishes. I'd stood in for both Elijah and Ahab at the lighting rehearsal, so I hadn't actually seen what it looked like from the audience, but it certainly sounded what Bill would call terribly-dramatic.

It was going so well that I couldn't help looking round to see whether Angel was still putting her curse on the show, and she wasn't. At least she'd gone. I turned to see Jake coming up the back steps with his arm held across his face and draped with a black cloth so that he'd stay invisible till his cue. The garden song was just ending when Angel came stamping up the side steps, strode across to the handmaid in green and silver and dragged her to the edge of the stage where Danny could see. Only then did she rip off the headscarf.

I think Juan had been completely taken by surprise. He didn't seem to realise what was happening until he felt the headscarf go. Then he tried to tug his arm free and at the same time aimed a savage kick at Angel's ankle, which must have hurt him more than her as he was barefoot and she was wearing boots. If it did, he didn't show it. He stopped struggling and drew himself up, staring down to where Danny lay. His lips were scarlet, his cheek blobbed with its garish circle, his eyes ringed with blue, but all at once it was impossible to believe that anyone could ever have mistaken him for a girl.

Chapter Eleven

"Oh you so much fools!" said Danny. "If you at the first give us the kid, not any of all this happen to you!"

"No," said Mum.

He hadn't expected an answer. His voice was even softer and slower than before, but he was really angry. He'd spent all day looked bored and listless, mostly lying on his bedding and letting Chip and Al run things. I'd thought he'd decided everything was hopeless and had pretty well given up, but now it felt as if he'd really been waiting, gathering strength for something tremendously important that was going to happen in the afternoon, and this was it. He was completely alive now, taut with energy and anger. He didn't need his gun to dominate us, or to seem very dangerous. It was worse because he didn't feel dangerous-mad, like Angel—he felt dangerous-sane. I was amazed when Mum interrupted him. She hates rows. She never disagrees with people outside the family if she can help it— that's one of the reasons why she gets so tensed up. I think even Danny was surprised. At any rate he waited for her to explain what she meant, but she just stood there, shaking her head.

"It wasn't like that," said Mrs Banks. "People with guns bursting in, looking for a child. Of course you hide him. It's all you can do. The rights and wrongs don't matter."

"The rights and wrongs not matter?" purred Danny, still talking to Mum as though Mrs Banks had just been interpreting for her. "You are all the same. You think you do all that you wish and it is OK because you buy with your money a big space all round you where you say there is no right and no wrong, only what you want must happen there. But you are fools. In everything there is right, there is wrong. When you accept this boy to play in your opera, you make the opera one wrong. When your government try to become a friend to Colonel Vanqui, then all you rich people, you who never have one thought of Matteo, still you begin to breathe a bad air. What your government does is like a bomb, a nuke, far off. In Matteo it hurts many people, but you think it does not hurt you safe in England. Fools, I say. Now, yes, now, without knowing, you are breathing the small small dust which will lie in your lung and make one day the cancer."

He said all this straight to Mum, who stared at him as though he was talking a foreign language. I don't know why he chose her—she'd only spoken one word—but he seemed to have decided she was the chief criminal. From his point of view, I suppose she was—I mean if there'd ever been a real disagreement in the mafia I think it would have been Mum who had the final say—but I don't see how Danny could have known that.

"It was I who hid the boy," said Mrs Dunnitt in her croaking voice, so flat that she sounded as though she was discussing what to cook for supper. "I know about Matteo. I was against having him in the opera. But I would hide him again. I did the opposite once, and I was wrong."

Danny blew out a long breath, snorting the argument away, and started in again about the hypocrisy of the bourgeois class. I'm afraid I stopped listening. I was getting more and more scared, not by what he actually said but the way he said it. He seemed to be working himself up to something, something he was going to do, not just talk about—the next gesture. I mean, there wasn't even any good practical reason why he should have got the mafia up onto the stage and bawled us out in front of the children. He needed the audience, that's all.

And it wasn't as if we were in a much worse mess than we'd been before, in fact finding Juan might actually make things easier—

there wasn't anything the bandits could do to us they couldn't
have done before, and now we didn't have the everlasting nervy
business, on top of all the other horrors, of keeping Juan hidden
and wondering what would happen if they found him. I'm afraid
it even crossed my mind that now they'd got Juan they might let
the rest of us go, but as soon as I thought about it I realised they
couldn't afford to. We were their only weapon—or rather the
children were. Though the church couldn't possibly have been
defended in a real siege, with its seven doors and thirty-odd
windows, the people outside simply couldn't risk an attack like
they'd done at the Iranian Embasssy siege. After all, a couple of
hostages had got killed there, hadn't they? But they'd been
adults, and foreigners—it's awful saying that, but it's true. Even
the SAS wouldn't manage to look like heroes if twenty or thirty
English children came out dead.

So, I decided, things hadn't changed all that much. We'd been
here before—last night. This was just going to be another of
those bad patches when everybody's right on edge and the
whole thing seems as if it's about to blow up, but it won't
provided we're sensible. By bedtime we'd all have simmered
down and be back where we were this morning.

I was wrong. Everything changes. You are never really back
in exactly the same place. You can never be sure, when
something starts happening all over again, that it's not suddenly
going to swing off those old tracks and go plunging along a line
you'd never even realised was a possibility. I began to see this
when Danny let us go at last and told us to pack twenty of the
children into the aisle in front of the hide and then sit ourselves
with the others in the front pews. I found the children had a
stunned, empty look, and they didn't seem to understand what
we were telling them to do. They knew we weren't allowed to
talk, but they kept whispering questions.

"What'll they do to Juan?"

"I don't know. Shh. Nothing."

"Are they going to kill him?"

"For God's sake stop talking and sit down . . . It's all right, honestly, I'm doing my best."

(That last bit to Angel who was in the hide now. She'd got a new trick. She'd make her beads do their warning rattle and then in the silence she'd do something with her gun which made one sharp metallic click. You froze, because it sounded like a last warning—the safety-catch—the next noise would be the bang of bullets, and then the screams.)

When we'd got them settled at last they were still restless. Danny paid no attention. He spent a long time on the telephone. I could hear he was having an argument, but there seemed to be a lot of silences. Juan sat on the floor by his knee. Danny had made him change into jeans and a T-shirt and sweater and then lashed a length of sash-cord (Mr Slim gets through miles of it every year) round his waist and the other end round his own wrist, just like Long John Silver did with that boy in *Treasure Island*. I began to understand how the children felt, and why they were so shocked and shaken when Juan was found. Until now hiding him had been a sort of game, almost, and we'd been winning. More than a game, a secret battle, like those films about digging tunnels out of POW camps under the noses of the German guards. While that lasted there had been something to feel inwardly hopeful about, a bit of the battle in which we were winning. Now there was nothing.

On top of that I'm sure the children felt it was all the mafia's fault. Of course it wasn't. Mrs Dunnitt had done marvels getting Juan disguised, and once he'd got through the first parade it would have been madness to try and find some other way of hiding him—for one thing he simply had to stay with the rest of us to get fed—no way could we have sneaked meals up into the gallery or somewhere. Maybe we shouldn't have let the rehearsal go ahead, but it hadn't seemed that dangerous, and honestly I still don't know what it was about Juan that had made Angel spot he was a boy. You can't say it takes a woman to see things like that, because I'm one too, for God's sake, and I hadn't seen anything wrong. For all that, I felt that the children, who'd been marvellously biddable so far, had now stopped trusting us.

For more than an hour we sat dreary and aching. Nothing changed, except that the daylight behind the windows turned slowly from white to grey, then shot into white again as the outside floods came on. Quite soon another night would have begun. Danny had finished his telephone call and listened to the news bulletins a couple of times. When Al took Angel's place in the hide Danny came and had a short discussion with him. Then he untied Juan's cord from his wrist and lashed it round the pillar near the right-hand edge of the dais. He gave Juan a kneeler to sit on.

After that Danny spent some time walking to and fro on the dais in front of the stage. He still gave me that feeling of working himself up towards some big event, and being determined to show he wasn't impatient for it to happen. He went off again to huddle over the radio, listening to the four-o'clock bulletin with the volume turned right down. When he came back he climbed onto the stage and clapped his hands. He needn't have done that. We were all silent already, all watching.

"OK," he said. "Now I tell you a little more about the camps where my friends are living. In some camps it is not so bad. In some camps very bad. Now we pretend you are my friends, living in this not so bad camp. OK? Food comes to this camp every day. The guards, they hit you only a little, when you are not quick to do the orders. And the guards take trouble so that every day you prisoners make exercise. In one big circle you must walk, round and round, not talking, all one hour. Now we will do this, so that you know more what it is like to be my friends, living in these camps. After that the food comes. If anybody talk, or is bad in any way, no food for them. Understand? So, out of this bench, begin. Go this way."

Believe it or not, it was an incredible relief. I'd never have thought it would be possible to enjoy shuffling up the south side-aisle, across in front of the stage, down the north aisle, back towards the south door and up the south aisle again. It ought to have been utterly boring and frustrating because it was impossible to keep a steady pace. You couldn't help behaving like traffic on a busy motorway, sometimes bunching until you could only inch along and sometimes opening up until you could move at almost a proper walk. If you looked across the church you could actually see it happening on the other side. It was just like watching one of those bristly caterpillars moving along—its ripples make the bristles close up and spread out in a steady pattern all along its length. Danny didn't help by insisting on controlling the flow across in front of the stage so that there were always at least a dozen of us in Al's firing-line.

We'd kept this up for about a quarter of an hour when Danny clapped his hands and called "Stop!"

We all stood still.

"Now I think we do something new," said Danny. "I think we have some music for your exercise. I know you all make the very good music, I hear it. But now only one person will play. It is so in the camps sometimes. One prisoner play and the others march. Who play for us now?"

Because of the way we'd come out of the pews the mafia were in one group together, close to where Danny was standing. They hesitated, looking at each other. Most of the orchestra were in a separate group down in the cross-aisle.

"Quick!" said Danny.

"Elsie, dear?" said Mrs Banks.

"What?" said Mum.

"Will you play something for us?"

"If you really want me to," said Mum.

Her voice was dreamy—in fact she sounded a little drunk— but she moved out of the line and over to the orchestra area in front of the side-chapel.

"OK, march!" called Danny.

There was a jam in the north aisle. We inched down it. I was

half-way across the church when I heard the long boom of the
bass string of the Testori. The hair on my nape prickled at the
sound. Of course like everyone else I'd expected Mum simply to
sit down at the piano and tonk out something cheerful like *Men
of Harlech*—I'd never thought of her using her cello, but next
time I crossed in front of the stage, there she was bent over the
glossy wood, head cocked a little to listen to the note as she
tuned, but body almost like a foetus huddled in the womb. It was
another full circuit before she was happy with the tuning. I heard
the two lower strings going down and down so I knew she was
going to play the Kodaly. She started somewhere in the middle
of the slow movement, and I realised that that must have been
where she'd got to, playing in her head.

I won't try and describe Kodaly's *Sonata for Unaccompanied
Cello*, but there are two things about it which even a completely
unmusical person must be able to hear, even if they've never
heard it before—it's a marvellous noise and it's incredibly
difficult to play. I think a lot of virtuoso music's a bore, just
show-off doodling, but the Kodaly isn't like that. If you want to
hear a cello really sing, listen to the slow movement. But even
then you'll find yourself gasping at some of the tricks the cellist
has to bring off—there are places where if you shut your eyes
you'll find it difficult to believe there isn't at least a trio playing.
On top of that the two lower strings have to be tuned down to
increase the range, which makes the fingering different from
normal. It's the sort of piece where it's no use only your mind
knowing the music, your fingers have to know it too. For some
reason there isn't much solo cello music, but if the Kodaly (and
the Bach suites, I suppose) were all there was it would still be a
terrific solo instrument.

Mum used to play the Kodaly quite often, sometimes at
recitals but mostly just for herself. It's as though it was a
talisman, a proof to herself that while she could still play it she
was still a professional musician. So she knew it—mind and
heart and fingers—but even so it was pretty odd to hear it then,

there. Though it was nothing like marching music it was lovely
to listen to, and for several turns round the church I hardly
noticed whether we were shuffling inch by inch or walking
properly. I looked at her each time round but we might not have
been there. She was completely absorbed in playing, sucked into
the music like water into a sponge. That's terrific, I thought—a
real bit of luck. I knew she'd been feeling the strain of the siege,
probably worse than any of us, because she had to bottle it all
up. She couldn't scream or weep or even try to tell anyone what
she was feeling so the tension inside her had simply been getting
worse and worse. But now she was working it out, playing the
Kodaly—that's one of the things music is supposed to be for,
after all.

About the fourth time round I saw that Danny had moved
away from the edge of the stage and was watching her play,
though he was still keeping half an eye on us to make sure there
were enough people crossing in front of the hide all the time.
Next time, as I came up the south aisle, I saw that he was saying
something to her. He was holding forth—another harangue
about bourgeois art, I guessed—but she'd didn't seem to have
heard him. She was into the last movement now, which is jiggy,
flickering, full of fireworks. It needs incredible speed and
precision—you couldn't possibly think about anything else
while you were playing it. In fact I thought Mum was having a
bit of trouble anyway. She must have been pretty well exhausted
before she started, but just as I turned the corner the music
slurred and stopped completely. I pushed out of line onto the
dais steps so that I could see round Mr Slim and find out what
had happened.

Danny had laid his hand across the strings and half-closed his
fist, gripping the bow at the same time. Mum was still uncoiling
herself from her huddle and was beginning to stare up at him.
Her mouth was open. She looked completely dazed. I don't
suppose anything like that had happened to her since the
practical jokes at the Royal College. Everybody had stood still,

jostling into each other, when the music stopped, but Danny waved to us angrily with his pistol to go on moving. He started talking to Mum again. In a few more paces I could hear what he was saying.

"Why do you play like this?" he said. "Can you not see them?"

He flung out a pointing arm towards us. Mum just shook her head.

"These are your friends, your daughter. They are in danger, they are afraid, they suffer. But you play like they are not there. It is for them you must make your music. If you do not, then I tell you . . . I tell you it is all crap!"

I couldn't stand it. I mean, I could understand what he meant and I can see it's a point of view—in fact Adam often says the same sort of thing when he's in the mood—but saying it to Mum—stopping her playing in order to say it . . .

I'd just reached the corner by the orchestra-space. Mum and Danny were only a few feet away. Instead of turning I went straight on up to him.

"Lay off," I said. "You don't know what you're talking about. Mum's a bloody good player. You're lucky to have heard her. And what's more anything she does is a bloody sight more important than anything you and your stupid friends get up to."

He flicked his pistol at me.

"Go back in the line," he said. "You get no food."

I looked at Mum. She knew who I was, I think. At any rate she smiled at me as if she was seeing me from a long way away.

"Play us some nursery rhymes, darling," I said. "Like you used to."

"Go back in line or your mother has no food," said Danny.

"Going," I said.

As I went down the north aisle Mum started into *Lavender's Blue*. I wished she hadn't chosen that one. When I was small the au pair would wash my hair and I'd go down and dry it in front of the drawing-room heater and Mum would stop practising and play nursery rhymes and I would sing. *Lavender's Blue* was always my favourite. Even on ordinary days I can't think of it without getting a bit of a lump in my throat.

We trudged round for another half hour while Mum worked her way through *Mother Goose*. At last the telephone rang. Danny let it throb away for a couple of minutes, though I was pretty sure he was itching to pick it up, but just by not answering he was exercising his will, controlling whoever was trying to get him from the far end. At last he picked up the handset, listened briefly, said a couple of words and rang off. He clapped his hands. We stopped walking.

"Enough," he said. "Now I think you know a little more about the camps. Sit on the benches. When you are quiet you will be given food. No food for Doll, who is bad."

I didn't mind all that much. It's when you've got absolutely nothing to do except sit still and be bored and frightened you think a lot about your next meal. It's the same in hospitals, and I'm sure it is in the real camps. It's not just because you're hungry. Places like that tend to turn you into a kind of unperson —sometimes because they want to, sometimes because they can't help it—but when you are eating you become a person again. It's something nobody else can do for you. I wasn't really hungry, and I suppose by stepping out of line and bawling out Danny I'd done my bit about becoming a person. Anyway, my mouth hardly watered while I helped take the food round— bread and cheese and an apple and a plastic cup of water. Almost all the children tried to sneak me a corner of their ration, but I smiled and shook my head. I knew Danny would be watching, and I wanted him to see me refusing to cheat—choosing not to. It was another kind of being a person. (I suppose, if you were in a real camp, cheating would become very important, not because of anything you got out of it but because it was a way of defeating the people who were trying to unperson you.)

We'd just about finished that when the telephone rang again. Danny answered it almost at once, listened and rang off without a word. I was on my way back to my pew when he came lounging over and jerked his head about a tenth of an inch to tell me he wanted me to follow him. I was learning. He wasn't as cool as he made out, anything like. The nearer we got to a crisis point the more effort he made to hide his nerves and act the calm professional, so now the actual smallness of his gesture told me that he was inwardly seething with excitement. Chip was waiting for us by the south door. I went through the drill of getting into the porch and having a gun pointed at me.

It was different this time, because usually Mr Slim or one of the mafia had been with me, but at first not all that different. When Danny opened the outer doors I couldn't see anything beyond the floods except two faint lines of pearly blobs—the lights of Dryden Avenue—fading off into utter dark; but I could sense a vague stir of movement, not because there were more people outside than before but because something was about to happen. A man appeared suddenly—like a trick, like Elijah materialising in Naboth's vineyard—and walked towards me. I could see he wasn't a policeman. It was his walk, brisk enough but somehow still a bit languid. He might have been a soldier once, but not any longer. He stopped outside the doors.

"May I come in?" he said.

His voice told me. He was what Granny Tope would call "one of us. " For instance, he could easily have been one of the opera fathers, or one of Dad's colleagues from the Ministry who sometimes come to dinner and because they've got it into their heads we're a musical family insist on talking about the late Beethoven quartets. (I don't mind the quartets, but the talk about them!)

"OK. In. Quick," said Danny from behind his door.

The man stepped into the porch. As Danny and Chip closed the doors and shut out the silhouetting glare I saw that he was tall, slim, about Dad's age, wearing an expensive brown suit. Grey hair—what was left of it—brushed into careful wings beside his temples. A big beaky nose and not much of a chin.

He smiled at me as if he was feeling a bit shy, but I expect he was just nervous. Then Chip took my elbow and led me back into the nave. I helped him unhook and close one pair of swing doors.

"That your Lord Carrington?" he muttered to me.

"Who? Oh, no. *He* wears enormous specs. I suppose . . . No, I'm sure it's not. But if he's from the Foreign Office he's one of the top people."

"Jesus!" said Chip.

"Why? Danny can't have . . ."

"Can it, Doll," he said.

He stood quite still, except that the hand that wasn't holding the gun kept balancing up and down in front of the belt-buckle as if he was trying to guess the weight of the air on his palm. I could hear the voices beyond the swing doors but not words. It was mostly Danny, interrupting the other man, who kept trying to say something. After only two or three minutes of this Danny called.

"C'mon," said Chip.

I stood in the usual place and the usual things happened while they let the stranger out. He smiled at me again but he looked angry and worried. As soon as the doors were shut Chip said, "Sit back in your place, baby," and I went off, leaving them talking in low voices in Spanish.

You can't stay in a state of utter tension for longer than a certain time. However bad things are, something in your system finds a way of letting in a bit of slack. Even excitement becomes boring in the end. I started to think. Danny had been working up to a crisis all day, and in his own mind it was going to be his interview with the Foreign Secretary. I was pretty sure that what I'd told Chip had been true—the bloke we'd seen had been a high-up in the FO —but that wasn't good enough for Danny. I was sure the FO couldn't actually have promised him he'd be seeing Lord Carrington, but he must somehow have believed he would. It was almost the same as what had happened during the broadcast last night—he'd expected too much, because he was an amateur, and now he felt cheated. A professional would have realised he'd be lucky to get a quarter of what he asked for, but Danny still wanted his crisis, his high point, Danny versus Mr Big, and it hadn't happened.

What would he do? Something. It wasn't much use trying to remember what had happened in other sieges, because the people who'd started them had been at least half-professionals. They'd gone in knowing roughly what they were up to, and how they planned to react if various things happened. At the Iranian Embassy it had got as far as the bandits saying they were going to start shooting hostages, then firing some shots to make it look as though they had, and then, when nothing happened, really doing it, and throwing the body out into the street. I couldn't believe Danny would shoot children, but there were nineteen adults too. They'd start with a man, surely. Toby. Bill. One of the orchestra. Mr Slim.

I couldn't believe that either—not yet. All the same I was absolutely sure Danny wouldn't let the whole crisis subside. The pressure was there. He'd been building it up all day, in himself, in the whole chain of happenings around him. Somehow he was going to make it explode.

The telephone started to ring. Chip and Danny moved up and stood beside it, still talking, letting it ring and ring so that the church once more became a great tooth aching with the sound of it. They seemed to be having an argument, and I thought perhaps they were using the noise of the telephone to stop the listening devices outside catching what they were saying. Once or twice Chip laid a hand on Danny's arm as if he was trying to calm him down. Angel joined them, looking sleepy and sulky. She leaned against the wall saying nothing. After a while Chip came over to the hide and took Al's place. Al joined the other two. Danny started to explain something to him. Al was reluctant and made objections, but Angel joined in, suddenly

looking pleased and interested. In the end Al agreed, but still
didn't look happy about it.

The telephone went on ringing unanswered while Danny and
Al strolled off to the back of the church and did something in the
porch. After a minute they came back with a chair and the small
table Mrs Talati uses for the tickets. These they took up onto the
front of the stage. Angel followed them up and Danny made
rather a business of handing over the automatic weapon he'd
taken from Al. Angel sat on the chair and banged the gun down
on the table.

She stayed there, staring grimly out over our heads while
Danny and Al fetched three more chairs and put them on the
dais in front of the stage, two rather to one side and one on the
other. I felt us all relax, breathe, perk up. They were so clearly
setting things up for some kind of performance for our benefit.

Looking back it seems quite extraordinary—absolutely crazy,
in fact—for them to take the risk, just the four of them with that
great church to guard and all of us to control and hundreds of
armed police outside waiting for the smallest mistake. All I can
say is it didn't seem crazy at the time. In fact it seemed somehow
logical. The point was Danny had to do something, or he'd
explode. I guessed he'd actually planned something much more
hairy and Chip had talked him out of it. He could have his
gesture but it wasn't to be a great big bloody one, not yet. It was
going to be a private gesture, a show, in which Danny could be
chief actor and parade and harangue to his heart's content, and
let the pressure down until it was safe for us all to start on
another night, another day.

Of course professionals would never have taken the risk, but
actually it wasn't anything like the risk it seemed. Everybody
—the bandits, us, the people outside—knew that as long as one
of the four was sitting in the hide with a loaded gun in his hands
and twenty kids to shoot at, there wasn't a damned thing anyone
could do to rescue us. The other three could do whatever they
fancied—go to sleep, sing madrigals, drink themselves stupid—

and it wouldn't make any difference. Really, I thought, seeing how things had gone so far this was about the best that could happen. Good old Chip. I forgave him the liberties he'd taken. He had his head screwed on.

At last Danny took the telephone off the hook. He told Mr Tolland to go and switch on the stage lights and then moved around the nave looking at the effect and calling out for alterations until he'd got what he wanted, one bright light on Angel, one on the dais immediately below her, and a less intense illumination on the three chairs. When he was satisfied he went up to the brightest area of the dais and raised his hands as if he was going to bless us.

"OK," he said. "This afternoon you make a show for us, and we learn from you. Now we make a show for you and you learn. The show we make is a trial, a justice court. First for a trial it is necessary there is the judge. It is not a judge like you have in England, a rich old man who is wearing robes and false hair. It is a judge of the people. See!"

He flung up an arm and pointed to Angel, who slowly picked her gun from the table and held it above her head, glaring out over our heads into the dimness of the nave.

"Good," said Danny. "Now there must be the advocates. For the people, I am the advocate. For the criminal . . . this will be a trial of full justice. You shall choose who shall be the advocate for the criminal."

He waited, looking amused. We shuffled on our seats. The children can't have had much idea what was happening.

"I suppose we'd better humour him," whispered Mrs Banks. "I should think Dave knows . . ."

"Oh, please not," said Mrs Slim. "I don't think he's up to it, are you, darling?"

"Well . . ." murmured Mr Slim. He really wasn't looking too good. I leaned across.

"If it's going to be about Matteo," I said, "Mrs Dunnitt . . ."

"Nancy?" said Mrs Banks.

Mrs Dunnitt sighed, got to her feet and edged out of the pew and up onto the dais. Some of the children began to whisper—a lot of them don't really like Mrs Dunnitt—she can be pretty brusque and alarming.

"Good," said Danny. "You choose well."

He made a fuss of showing Mrs Dunnitt to one of the two chairs on the left.

"Surely he's not going to try poor little Juan," whispered Mrs Slim.

"I should think he'll get that other thug to act this Blick person," said Mrs Banks.

She must have spoken loud enough for Danny to hear, because when he turned round I could see that he was almost purring with the fun he was going to have. He was playing with us, like Noggin with a bird. He came slowly towards us until he stood at the mouth of the centre aisle.

"Last," he said, "we must have the criminal. Who is it the people accuse?"

He drew himself up and tilted his head as though he was about to make a proclamation to an enormous crowd.

"It is you," he called. "The people accuse you. All you."

The echoes dwindled—*you, you, you.* Danny waited for them to die.

"Yes," he went on in a quieter voice. "All you. But you cannot all sit on one chair. This is a show we make, a play. In a play one actor is the representation of many people. Your Ahab, your Elijah, they are not themselves only, they are all men who have done such things or wished such things. So for our play we choose one actor who is the spirit of all you. One person, thinking no harm, staying easy and quiet while in Matteo terrible things are done, and for amusement making music, an opera for the children, yes? I think, my friends, we choose . . . we choose . . . you!"

He had been speaking more and more quietly, though he had the actor's trick of making a soft sound fill a large space. He snapped the last word in a way that made us all jump, and at the same moment his arm shot out, pointing to my left.

"Me?" whispered Mum. "Oh, no!"

Chapter Twelve

Mum was edging out of the pew—I'd just squeezed her hand as she passed me—when Mrs Dunnitt said in a loud voice "I refuse to participate."

Danny turned to her.

"I refuse to participate," she said again.

Danny went up onto the dais and turned towards us before he answered her. By doing so he made what she was saying somehow inside his performance, although Mrs Dunnitt meant it as a protest against it from the outside. He looked thoroughly pleased and interested.

"Yes?" he said encouragingly.

"I mistook your intentions," she said. "I thought this was to be a dramatised trial of the Blick regime. Instead you are trying to make it into something like a real trial, a show trial. One thing I have learnt over the years—one must never accept a show trial. It doesn't matter who is being tried or why— whether it's the Moscow purges, or Nuremberg, or Eichmann, if the trial is being used for propaganda, it poisons the springs of justice."

"But this trial is not real," said Danny. "It is a play, a drama. How can you say it is real?"

"Of course it's not fully real," said Mrs Dunnitt. "But the crucial element is real. If you had put the unspeakable Blick on trial you would have had an empty chair, or an actor to represent him. But now you are going to accuse Mrs Jacobs of things you will say she herself has done or not done. I want no part of it. I refuse."

Without waiting for an answer she strode off the dais. I was twisting my knees aside to let her along the pew when Mum stopped her.

"Please, Nancy," she said.

Mrs Dunnitt shook her head.

"You're the only person who can help me," said Mum.

Mrs Dunnitt looked at her and frowned.

"It's only a play, Mum," I whispered. "It isn't real."

She seemed not to hear me.

"Please, Nancy," she said.

Mrs Dunnitt glanced at me. I couldn't think what to do—I didn't even know what I felt. It seemed to me important that Danny should have his drama to stop something worse happening—if only it hadn't been Mum! She was in a complete daze—she sounded almost as if she thought she was having a very bad dream . . . in the end I just nodded. Mrs Dunnitt sighed, turned, and the two of them went up to the dais.

"Fine," said Danny, pointing to the two chairs. "Now we begin."

"I wish to make a statement," said Mrs Dunnitt.

Danny spoke in Spanish to Angel, who nodded. Mrs Dunnitt turned to us.

"Since this performance is apparently intended for your education," she said, "I will try to use it to educate you about the nature of political justice. If ever you find yourselves involved in anything of this sort in the real world, you have only one honourable course of action. You must refuse to accept the validity of the court. I hereby do so."

So Mum's "trial" started with a long argument about whether the court had any right to try her. I was really too upset for Mum to listen to it much. I wasn't just upset because of the state she was in, I was actually frightened for her. I couldn't help it. Although I kept telling myself this was only a stupid play to keep Danny happy, I couldn't help feeling it was somehow real, and that when Danny had found her guilty (I was sure he would) *then* he'd do something . . .

The children seemed to feel the same, somehow. They were extraordinarily quiet and interested, although the argument was pretty abstract, about what gives any court the right to try people. When Mrs Dunnitt scored a point you could sense them inwardly cheering, and when Danny scored they sighed with disappointment. The argument was a draw. Angel stopped it by rapping her gun on the table and asking Danny a question in Spanish. He went to the edge of the stage and spoke to her in a low voice while she craned down to listen. She straightened up and stared at us in silence for a moment, holding the gun tilted across her chest.

"The court . . . eesa . . . valida," she said. "Eesa court . . . of people."

I realised that till then, in all the time I'd been in the church, I hadn't heard her speak a word of English, not even "Sit down." Danny nodded as if he was pleased with the way she'd repeated her lesson, but I think he was pleased too with this twist in the drama—to have a trial where the judge could hardly understand a word that was being said . . . My mind slithered, leaped to something I'd thought of before. Suppose he was planning to put pressure on the people outside by threatening to kill one of us, who would he choose? How would he choose? A trial—a series of trials . . . was Mum the first . . . ?

I pushed the idea out of my mind. It was only a play—a stupid play.

Danny turned to Mum.

"OK, now we begin," he said. "What is your name?"

"One moment," said Mrs Dunnitt, "since we do not recognise the validity of the court we do not accept the decision."

Danny was about to speak again when Mum said, "Let's get it over, darling."

Mrs Dunnitt shrugged and sat down.

"What is your name?" said Danny again.

"Elsie Tope—I mean Jacobs," said Mum in a too-bright voice.

"You have two names?"

"I suppose so. Jacobs is my married name. Tope is my professional name. I'm a professional musician—a cellist."

"Two names," purred Danny. "Very good."

He paused. I wondered whether he guessed the state Mum was in—whether he'd have minded if he knew. I suppose when his friends had been tried in Matteo—*if* they'd been tried—they were often in pretty poor nick, after what the police had done to them to get them ready for the trial.

"OK," said Danny. "Two names, two criminals, two charges, yes? We charge the prisoner Jacobs. She is a bourgeois housewife. During eight years the criminal Blick has murdered and tortured the Matteo people. For this he needs the economic support of the capitalist countries, buying his sugar and his bananas, all which he makes the Matteo people slaves to grow for him. Those who buy these foods assist the criminal Blick in his murders and tortures. Do you say guilty or not guilty?"

Mum looked at Mrs Dunnitt, who rose.

"Since we do not recognise the court we cannot plead guilty or not guilty,"

"Darling," said Mum, "I think . . ."

Danny gave an impatient snort. Mrs Dunnitt didn't seem to mind.

"But suppose we were to recognise the court, which we do not," she said, "my client would then plead Not Guilty."

"OK," said Danny. "Now the Prisoner Tope. During eight years, as I tell you, the criminal Blick murders and tortures the Matteo people. The duty of the artist is to the people. In all the world artists are doing this duty, speaking for the people, painting and playing music for the people, and also sending money for the revolution of the people. Each artist who does not do this, he betrays his art and he betrays the people. And when this prisoner Tope make music for the ambassadors in white shirts and women who have diamonds in their hair, she gives support to the criminal Blick so he thinks he may make more murders. In especial, when she accepts into this opera the nephew of the criminal Vanqui, she gives support to Vanqui and Blick. What do you say?"

"Again, hypothetically, not guilty," said Mrs Dunnitt.

"OK. First, for the people the witness is Al."

Now, suddenly, just like the opera taking off, the "trial" came alive. Al told us a lot of perfectly horrible things about Matteo. He'd been the priest of some villages which supplied workers to a big sugar plantation. He told us how his people had lived, like animals, and badly kept animals at that. The plantation belonged to a company which was partly owned by an American sugar company and partly by rich Matteans who supported President Blick. In the end there'd been a strike, which Al had helped to organise. The Mattean army came to break the strike with American helicopters and tear-gas and rifles and tanks. They'd killed several hundred people and arrested a lot more, including women and children. Then they'd tortured them. Al told us exactly what they'd done to him. He said they weren't even pretending to try and find things out from him, they just tortured him because that was what they did. In the end he was let out for the same reason as Chip had been but not at the same time.

Al spoke pretty fair English but he wasn't actually very good at describing things, and he obviously hated talking about the worst horrors, but that made it all the more effective when Danny got it out of him. Sometimes on TV you see a report about that sort of ghastliness, or about some frightful famine which nobody's bothering to cope with, and the awful thing is how you get bored with the way they rub it all in—you resent being got at like that, especially by fat cat reporters who are paid thousands and thousands to fly off to some hell-hole and bring back a documentary on the shanty-towns when you're pretty sure that the moment they've got their film in the can they'll be back on the patio of the only posh hotel, watching the silk-skinned lovelies in the swimming-pool and knocking back Scotch at twenty quid a bottle on expenses. (I know about that because it's what Nick Wintle's dad does for a living, though I've never met him personally—Nick's parents split when he was tiny and Pa Wintle has been married twice more, at least.) Somehow what Al told us wasn't a bit like that. You felt it all. It wasn't because you were bored you wanted him to stop. Your skin didn't seem to get any thicker as horror followed horror.

At last Danny said, "Thank you" and turned to Mrs Dunnitt.

"You accept these evidences?" he said. "You want that I bring more witnesses?"

Mrs Dunnitt and Mum had a confab. I couldn't see Mum's face at all. She kept making puzzled little gestures with her right arm and cutting them short. I could see Mrs Dunnitt when she leaned forward but I couldn't read her expression. I guessed she was feeling very uncomfortable—I mean, in spite of what she'd said about refusing to accept the court she was actually more serious about the trial than anyone on our side. Matteo mattered to her. She agreed with Danny about President Blick, and so on. One of my godfathers is a QC who gets enormous fees by defending big criminals. He's got a special line in the sort of thug who clobbers security-guards and scoots off with the wages van, sometimes actually shooting people in the process. My god-father is so totally mild and civilised to meet that it's almost funny, but of course he takes a pretty smooth line about his thugs—he says justice can't operate unless the best possible case is made for both sides, so somebody has to do it for what looks like the rotten side, otherwise once in fifty times, when the police have collared the wrong lot of thugs, justice will fail. I couldn't see Mrs Dunnitt feeling quite so detached about it all.

The "judge"—Angel—rapped her gun on her table as if she was getting impatient. Mrs Dunnitt stood up.

"We do not dispute the evidence in principle," she said. "By that I mean that some of the details may be mistaken or exaggerated, but we accept that most of them are true, and that

the Blick regime has perpetrated many similar outrages. But I
have some questions to ask."

"What questions?"

"You will hear them. You can object then."

Danny hesitated, then spoke to Angel in Spanish. She'd been
getting bored, I thought, but now she cheered up.

"OK, we do it this way," said Danny. "You whisper to me
the question. I explain to the judge. She decide if you ask the
question."

Mrs Dunnitt smiled her thin smile.

"I thought this performance was supposed to portray a court
of justice," she said. "Where is the justice if the questions of the
prosecution go unchallenged, but the questions of the defence
have to have the permission of the court?"

They argued about it for several minutes but in the end Mrs
Dunnitt gave way, and again I heard that strange tennis-court
sigh all along the pews. It really seemed to matter. You got a
feeling of being pushed back, squeezed in, cornered—and each
time you felt as though we were being nudged a little nearer the
point at which whatever was going to happen would really have
to be faced. In fact Angel let Mrs Dunnitt ask all her questions.
They were partly about British business interests in Matteo—
not much, apparently—and partly about an affair two years
earlier when the revolutionaries had kidnapped a British bank-
manager and the Blick regime had refused to let the bank
ransom him but the British had got round that somehow.
There'd been a real diplomatic hoo-ha about it and we'd made
ourselves thoroughly unpopular with Blick. Put like that it
sounds quite good, but Al was fairly scornful about it all. Mrs
Dunnitt got out of him that practically all the Mattean sugar
went to the USA, especially since we'd joined the Common
Market. He didn't know about fruit exports.

"OK," said Danny when she'd finished. "I must thank you
for not making long questions. It is time that Al sleep. And
because you are accepting his evidence of the crimes of Blick it is

not necessary to bring more witnesses to prove these things. So who will be the new witness? I think it will be the boy O'Grady."

I gulped—I don't know why—and I heard Mrs Slim whisper, "Oh, no!" That made it worse—I mean knowing that she was taking the silly business seriously too. Another argument started between Danny and Mrs Dunnitt. All this while Juan had been sitting on his kneeler, tied to the pillar, and looking as bored and disdainful as he knew how. Danny now loosed the pillar end of the cord and led him up onto the dais, but Mrs Dunnitt refused to go on until he was completely untied and given a chair to sit on. This time Mrs Dunnitt won her part of the argument, but then a much worse row broke out between Danny and Angel, in Spanish. Angel was absolutely furious at the idea of untying Juan, but I think Danny realised he couldn't afford to treat him like an animal in front of all the other children, and he'd get much more mileage out of seeming friendly and uncle-ish. Angel clattered her beads and snarled and slammed her gun on the table until Danny reached up and took it from her and ostentatiously checked that the safety-catch was set. (Incidentally that told me I'd guessed right about what she was doing to produce that metallic click from it.)

When he handed it back she snatched it from him and almost hugged it to herself—just like a child in a tantrum over a toy— and as Danny turned away she took it right down onto her lap, where she continued to fiddle with it out of sight. But Danny seemed to regard the argument as settled, so he untied Juan and put his own chair under the centre light for him. Juan must have understood what was being said during the argument with Angel but he'd made a great show of paying no attention, standing with his hands tied behind him and his head thrown back, proud and haggard, Our Hero facing the firing squad. I suppose it was mean of me to see him like that but I couldn't help it. Even if there'd been a real firing squad, he'd still have been playing that romantic role—pretty brave, when you think about it—much better than I'd have managed. He tried to keep it up while Danny questioned him, but it didn't look so heroic sitting down.

"You are Juan O'Grady?"

Juan turned his head a little further away and said nothing.

"Your father is the Ambassador of Matteo in England?"

Still no answer. Danny didn't seem at all put out.

"For a South American O'Grady is a strange name."

Juan glanced at him and away.

"Of course in Matteo it is not strange. I think every Matteo child know how one Irishman comes to Matteo in eighteen hundred nineteen . . ."

"Eighteen hundred and seventeen," said Juan scornfully.

"OK. Seventeen. The hero Juan O'Grady."

"Sean," said Juan, pronouncing the name the proper way— Shawn. "Captain Sean O'Grady, Twenty-third of foot."

"Why does he not stay in Ireland?" said Danny. "He has made himself a good name in the wars with Napoleon. He is of good ancient family, I think."

Danny had hit exactly the right note. For all his resolution Juan couldn't resist the chance to tell us about his hero-ancestor. He began to speak almost in a sing-song, sounding much more Spanish than usual. I guessed the words were something he knew by heart, but in Spanish.

"O'Grady was a Catholic," he said. "While he was fighting the French the English Earl Bagstock cheated him of his estate. When he came home from the war the Protestant lawyers cheated him of justice. They took all the money that was his. He came to Matteo with ten sovereigns and his sword."

"Ten sovereigns and his sword," echoed Danny, almost as if the words had been the chorus of a nursery rhyme. "And in six years with that sword he has driven the Spanish armies from Matteo. Our country is for the first time free. We share this story—all Matteo people share it. It is in our blood. The English did not much help him, I think."

"Not one dollar," said Juan, still saying his lesson. "Not one bullet. Bolivar they sent money and guns. San Martin they sent money and guns, but the enemies of O'Grady were strong in England. They were scared he would come back to Ireland with his sword of freedom."

Danny smiled. His eyes glittered. I think he really did feel excited by the story of Juan's ancestor—perhaps he saw himself one day doing almost the same.

"Blick is also for a South American a strange name," he suggested.

"Swedish," said Juan. He snorted the word so that for a moment I didn't get it—I thought it was some sort of Mattean swear-word.

"Swedish," repeated Danny. "I think it was the father of our President Blick who comes first to Matteo, but he does not bring his sword."

Juan looked at him from half-closed eyes. When he spoke it was still as though he was repeating words he'd learnt from adults, but this time they had a different tone. It took me a while to guess where he'd picked them up.

"Old Blick came with money-bags," he said. "He made a pile of money selling guns to Germany for the First Big War, but he cleared out when he saw they were going to lose. The President was not born in Matteo. They had to change the constitution so he could become President."

"Why is it worth the trouble?" said Danny. "Is there not a Matteo man fit to become President?"

"Money-bags," said Juan. "The Yankee bankers put him in."

I got it then—servants. Nobody I know has servants now, not counting au pairs, but four or five still have the old family nanny, either living with them or dropping in to darn socks and things, plump, slow biddies who have scolded two or even three generations through the same nursery. I've heard them say things a bit like Juan was saying now—of course he'd have been brought up among lots of servants, listened to their gossip, seen more of them than his parents. This was their talk, sharp and cynical. Even Danny seemed a bit surprised.

"Someone teach you good politics," he said. "It is not only the Yankee bankers, of course. There are big bankers in London, uh?"

"I suppose so."

"What is your father doing in London?"

"He's the Ambassador."

"Sure, but what is his work? It is to keep the English always the friends of President Blick, I think."

"Yes."

"What must he do for this?"

"Oh, I guess he gives receptions at the embassy, concerts, little dinners, you know. Sometimes he arranges for bigwigs to go on trips to Matteo, everything paid. I keep at him to get our football teams over, but it's always stupid dancers. When I am President . . ."

"I think your uncle, Colonel Vanqui, will be President first."

"Course he will."

"And he will want the English to be still his friends? You think he will buy English tanks, English fighters?"

"This summer I went for a ride in a Chieftain."

"A Chieftain tank? You are a lucky boy. Very lucky that you are behind the gun of this tank, and not in front of it. The English are trying to sell this tank to Blick?"

"I guess so."

"Good. Now, to end. Why is your father wishing you to be in this opera?"

Juan, who had been leaning forward, making man-of-the-world gestures to emphasise what he said, drew back and turned away, watching Danny out of the corner of his eyes. His mouth set shut.

"Many many important English people live in this place," said Danny. "Their kids are in this opera. I think your father says 'Go into the opera, be a friend with the kids of these people, so they think good about Matteo.'"

Juan looked right away. Beneath the smeared make-up I could see he was furious with sudden shame. Mrs Dunnitt coughed for attention.

"If I could ask a question," she said, "it might clarify the issue."

"OK, OK, I finish," said Danny.

He left his chair for her but she didn't sit down.

"Did you come to the opera last year, Juan?" she said.

"Yeah," he answered, not looking at her and trying to sound bored.

"What did you think of it?"

"Not bad."

"Did you decide you'd like to be in it?"

He shrugged, not willing to admit he'd wanted anything from us.

"When you told your mother what did she say?"

"She wasn't keen."

"But you got your way in the end?"

"Sure. She's only a woman. I went on at her."

"Thank you very much. That's all."

Danny was taken by surprise. He was leaning against the upper stage, whispering to Angel, rather obviously paying no attention to anything Juan might have to tell Mrs Dunnitt, when he became aware of the silence and turned. Angel straightened and threw back the hair which had fallen over her face. Her beads made a noise like a man snapping his fingers.

Then there was the business of tying Juan up again, which took a minute or two. The children fidgeted in the pews. There were a lot of yawns. I wanted to yawn too, but with nerves more than boredom—in fact I'd been really interested finding out a bit more about Juan's name. When the twins used to tease him about being a thick Mick he'd either fought or ignored them, never explained. But now, just because Danny had made his talk with Juan so easy and open, it felt as though walls had been quietly closing in on us while we were looking out that way, and click, suddenly there wasn't anywhere to run. I noticed that when Danny had finished tying Juan to the pillar and came back into the spotlight he held himself more stiffly and spoke in a slower and deeper voice.

"OK," he said. "If this is a true court in Matteo, the trial lasts many days. Many many witnesses, arguings from twelve lawyers, etcetera etcetera. Here we must finish so that you may sleep. We miss all that and come towards the end. We ask the prisoner some questions, and then I make one small speech and Mrs Dunnitt make one small speech and the judge says what the court decide. Then finish. OK? The prisoner will please stand up."

Mum rose and turned a little towards us. She looked quite dreadful, yellow and shaky. I longed to jump up and yell at Danny to stop torturing her but there was a sort of barrier of nerves which stopped me. Mercifully Mrs Dunnitt had a go.

"I don't think my, er, client is up to this," she said. "If this were a real court, her lawyers would certainly argue for an adjournment on medical grounds. Surely as it's . . ."

Mum made a wild gesture, flinging out her right arm as though she was hitting someone with the back of her hand.

"No," she said. "Oh no. Let's get it over. I can manage."

"I am glad you say this," said Danny, smiling. "In Matteo I see my friends made to face trial when they have been too much tortured to stand."

"That's no argument," snapped Mrs Dunnitt, suddenly really angry. "If anything, the fact that it's something your opponents do should make you even more careful not to copy them."

"OK, OK, we are not doing it. She says she wishes to proceed. Look, I put a chair for her to hold."

He slid Mum's chair round so that she could grip the back-rest, like a prisoner gripping the rail of the dock. Yes, just like that. But it obviously helped, and as he questioned her she pulled herself more and more together. He went back to the stupid business of pretending that she was two people, so he started with a lot of questions about her being a housewife and supporting the Blick government by buying slave-grown fruit. It was a complete farce. I really mean that. If I hadn't been so nervy I would have ached with secret laughter. Poor old Danny. He hit one of those absolutely unpredictable problems which happen because people are all so different from each other. It was a bit like the moment when he'd missed Juan in the parade because of the children wetting themselves. It was pure bad luck, but somehow served him right.

He asked Mum about bananas. Apparently the main Mattean export to Europe is bananas. But Mum would never dream of buying bananas. She was brought up by Granny Tope to believe that nice people don't eat bananas. They were vulgar. The sort of people who ate bananas put the milk into their cups before the tea and called their front room the parlour. During the war bananas sometimes sold on the black market for a pound apiece, but when Granny Tope was actually given a whole bunch by a friend who'd brought them back from America she wouldn't let Mum or Uncle Steve touch them and gave them to her char instead. It's loony, but the whole thing's stuck; I actually quite like bananas, but I still feel guilty when I eat one. Of course Mum couldn't explain any of this to Danny in public, and he simply couldn't believe that she never bought bananas. It was hysterical—or it would have been—with Mum behaving as though Danny was nosing into her sex life and Danny reacting as though Mum was deliberately making a fool of him. Even when he gave up on bananas and switched to other things it wasn't much use, because of course Mum hasn't the vaguest idea where anything she buys comes from. She even told him that avocado pears only grew in Israel. In the end he realised that he was losing control, and decided to change tack.

"OK," he said. "Now I ask the questions for the prisoner Tope. This is much more important matter. I think you tell me you are musician."

"I play the cello," said Mum.

"You have many friends who are musicians also?"

"Quite a lot, yes."

"With them you play music? You make concerts?"

"Sometimes."

"Tell me."

Mum began to explain, talking jerkily, with a little gasp between every few words.

"Well, I belong to a group which gives three or four concerts in the summer, in gardens—that's for charity. I play in a quartet, mostly for our own amusement, but we get a few professional engagements. We broadcast twice last year. Occasionally—influenza epidemics and things like that—I stand in for a cellist in one of the regular orchestras—I'm still a member of the Musician's Union . . . Is that what you want to know?"

"You forget to say *this*," said Danny. "This opera you do now."

"Oh, of course," said Mum. "That's very important to me."

"Is for charity also, I think," said Danny.

"Yes, but . . . that isn't why . . . it's for itself. We do it for love."

"OK. And the other music you make? Sometimes for charity. Sometimes for money. Is that always for love also?"

"Oh, yes. Yes, I suppose so. Even when . . ."

"When you say this *for love*, what is it which you are loving?"

"Oh . . . the music . . . making it . . . hearing it . . ."

"You do not consider it is *yourself* which you are loving? *Yourself* which makes this music? *Yourself* which hears it?"

"It . . . it doesn't feel like that . . . I mean somebody's got to play, or there wouldn't be any music, surely?"

"OK. Now these concerts, this opera—who comes?"

"Anybody who wants to. The opera, it's mostly friends, or friends of friends, or people who live round here . . . It's a bit different with the concerts and quartets, I suppose."

"But never you ask who comes. They pay the money, they enter?"

"Yes. One year we had to throw a drunk out."

"OK. All these people—what says the music to them?"

"Does it have to . . . Oh, well, most of the music I play is classical. I suppose it all says something, but . . . I mean, if you could put what it says into words there'd be no point in it being music, would there? The opera's a bit different. I mean, it's got words, and . . . usually it's got what you might call a message, but . . . honestly, you'd better ask Bill. He wrote this one."

"I ask you. I ask what you are telling the world with your music."

"I don't . . . The only thing I can think of might be . . . well . . . that music's worth having, for it's own sake. That's all."

"That is all? Never that there is somewhere the starving of children, somewhere the murder of workers, the beating of slaves, the torture of the friends of freedom?"

"All I can say is that that sort of thing doesn't come into the kind of music I play. I mean not directly. I don't know why, but somehow messages make bad music, usually."

"Good message, bad music?"

"I'm afraid so."

"OK. I finish."

Mum had pulled herself together quite a lot during all this. When Danny sat down she actually turned to Mrs Dunnitt and waited for her questions.

"Just two things, Elsie," said Mrs Dunnitt. "Last April there was a gala at the Mattean Embassy to celebrate the fifteenth anniversary of President Blick's coming to power. Suppose your quartet had been asked to take part in it, what would you have done?"

"I don't know. It depends who'd asked me. I mean, if it was one of the quartet I'd have assumed he knew what he was doing. Otherwise . . . I'd probably have consulted my husband if I'd had any doubts . . . knowing what I know now, I wouldn't have dreamed of it, of course."

"And the other side? A concert for the relief of conditions in the prison camps, or for Amnesty's work in Matteo?"

"Oh, yes, of course. I've done Amnesty concerts before."

"But your general position is that you are entitled to play your music without always questioning who will hear it. You think of it as superficially neutral, but underneath a vague force for good. Where there are definite moral objections you are not prepared to perform?"

"Yes."

"That's all. I think . . ."

"Moment," said Danny, rising. "She asks good questions. Now, if I come saying to you, make me this concert to buy guns for the revolution, what you say?"

"No," said Mum. "Never. I couldn't bear it, whatever the cause—using music to help somebody kill someone else . . ."

"OK," said Danny. "Finish. Sit down please."

As soon as she sat Mum hunched herself into her chair. I'd been really rather cheered up by the way she'd coped with the questions, but now I guessed what an effort she must have found it. She didn't seem to be listening at all when Danny began his speech, and at first neither did I. You know that odd instinct you have that something's ending—for instance when you turn on the radio in the middle of a play, you can usually tell without even listening to the words whether it's going to finish in the next few minutes. I felt the same then. Waiting for the finish made it hard to think about anything else.

But after a while I found myself listening. It was difficult not to, because of the way Danny was putting himself over to the children. He was talking to them about war.

"You do not remember—you are not born then," he said. "But on your television you see, often. Imagine. In your war, everything, everything is to fight the Germans. The food on your table is not food to give you joy, it is food to make you strong to fight. The games are to make your muscles strong, the lessons to make your minds clever, all to fight. On your famous BBC is often music, but always it is strong, soldier-music, full of hope. Or it is quiet, making for you pictures of the peace you will have when you win your war. Never is it no-hope music, never the songs of defeat. And this is right—you know this is right. You are proud your BBC is telling you the truth when the German radio is full of lies, but you do not think it is lies when the BBC plays music to make you brave and hopeful. So the music is the same as the food. It is the servant of your war.

"Now your war ends, you think. Peace. What you like you can eat. What music you wish you can play. There is perhaps a war somewhere, but you are neutrals, comfortable on this island. All your fight is to make for yourselves more money so you can become more comfortable . . .

"But I tell you, your war does not end. Never was true peace. While in this world, anywhere, one person is still a slave, is tortured, is in prison for what he has said, all nations are still at war, fighting for that one man. No neutrals, nowhere. Only fighters and traitors. When you do not join the fight, you betray. I have heard you sing in your opera the song of the King in the Middle. I tell you there is no middle. This king in your story is a traitor to the God in your story. So in this world, this real place which is not a story, you, and you, and you are traitors. You are traitors to Man."

Without shouting his voice filled every nook of the church, so that the echoes seemed to have nowhere to go but hung and muttered in the shadows. Sometimes he would drop almost to a whisper for a few phrases and then boom out again. He didn't really say anything he hadn't said before, and he didn't say much directly about Mum, apart from using her as an example to tell us what he thought of our whole social set-up, but it was all impressive and some of it was stunning. I think I would have been bowled over, despite being so tired and frightened, if his eyes hadn't gleamed in the spotlight and kept reminding me it was only a performance and he was loving it. I glanced round and caught Chip's eye. I think I saw his eyelid flicker. Good old Chip, I thought, organising things so that Danny could work out his frustrations at not being allowed the kick of negotiating with the Foreign Secretary. Perhaps we'd all get a decent night's sleep after this.

A few of the children were asleep already, but most of them were still wide awake, sitting very still, caught, hypnotised by Danny's performance. Angel too. She was leaning forward in her chair, mouth slightly open, staring at Danny with eyes so wide she might have been in some kind of trance. She couldn't have understood one word in three, but I guessed the meaning didn't matter—it was the voice, the excitement of sheer sound without sense working on her soul, the way some people think music does. At least she wasn't waving her gun around.

Danny finished. The last echoes whispered away while he stood motionless in the spotlight. A few of the children started to clap and the rest joined in. It wasn't just politeness. He'd really got through to them, I thought. Good. That would make him happier still.

When the clapping and cheering ended Danny made a courtly gesture towards Mrs Dunnitt and retired to his chair. Mrs Dunnitt stood up but didn't go into the spotlight.

"I'm not going to say very much," she said. "Just two things, one about justice and the other about Elsie's music. I told you earlier what I thought about show trials. As soon as you have a show trial, a symbolic accusation and sentence, you are making a parade of justice to suit other purposes, and to that extent the thing ceases to be justice. When the allies tried the Nazi leaders, when the Israelis tried the unspeakable Eichmann, they were trying criminals, but to the extent that these were show trials they were something other than justice. Now what are we to make of this so-called trial, in which a member of a supposedly offending group is picked at random, solely in order that there shall be a trial? The element of justice is not to my mind present at all. Everything that Danny has just said reinforces my conviction that I was right to advise Elsie to refuse to recognise the validity of this court. Any verdict it gives, any sentence it passes, will be worthless.

"My second point is about Elsie's music. I'd better start by saying that for almost fifty years I've been a soldier in Danny's war. I've fought its battles before he was born. My friends have been in prison, my husband died for it. I've been in prison myself—only for a short time and not a bad prison, so I won't make much of that. And in the course of this long war I've lived in a country—Russia—where there was no middle ground, nowhere for poor old Ahab to stand. All art served the cause, in the way Danny believes it should. A poet who wrote about the grass being green and the sky being blue was in disfavour unless she also wrote that it was thanks to the state that this was so.

"It is difficult for you to imagine what it must be like to live in a country like that, so I'm going to tell you a true story. I had a friend who was a poet, a very good poet, but she was in disfavour because she wrote about sky and grass, and love and death, and truth. Being in disfavour meant that she had no ration card and when her eyes got bad she had to use an old pair of spectacles which somebody had lent her. And of course her work never got published. But because she was a good poet her poems were passed from hand to hand, and copied, and passed on. And then, suddenly—I don't know why, some slip-up in the bureaucracy no doubt—she was allowed to give a public reading. The hall was packed. She read her poems. But because her spectacles were bad and because she was weeping so, she kept hesitating and stumbling. Every time she did so all the audience would prompt her. Every man, every woman in that big room knew her poems by heart. She was careful to read only about things like grass and sky—nothing controversial, not even truth. Next day the authorities took away even her borrowed spectacles and sent her to scrub floors in the Ministry of Labour.

"I must tell you one other thing about her. I said she was my friend. That's not quite true. I wanted her to be my friend, but I was afraid to admit to anyone that I liked her.

"Do you see what I am driving at? Danny has told you that he is fighting for justice and liberty in Matteo. So am I. So, I think, will many of you after what you have heard. But justice and liberty are not things that can be made to conform to anybody's will. I've tried to explain why a court such as this has little to do with justice, and now I'm trying to tell you how little liberty there is in a society which has no middle ground, no areas of neutrality. Art and poetry and music are only one kind of middle ground, one sort of freedom, but since they appear to be central to this so-called trial we must concentrate on them. A few weeks ago I was talking to Doll Jacobs about the other side of this question. We were discussing your friend Ferdy, the guard, whom I suspected of being one of Blick's secret police. Doll said he couldn't be, because he understood about the opera, and I told her about the commandants of Nazi extermination camps who had genuinely loved music. It was no excuse, I told her. Mozart cannot rescue such a man from damnation. But the other side to this also holds true—the admiration of such a man in no way degrades Mozart. Mozart is free. What is more, he is a part of all our freedom. So is Elsie's cello-playing. So is your singing in the opera. Those who claim to be fighting for freedom when . . . ''

She stopped. She'd been talking in a dry, steady voice. I suppose I should have realised she'd done quite a bit of public speaking in her time. She was pretty good at it, in a different way from Danny. You didn't need to look at her, you just wanted to listen to the plain words coming steadily out. In fact I was staring at the stitching of my jeans when she broke off in the middle of the sentence. I looked up to see why.

The judge's chair was empty. Angel was standing under the spotlight. Danny was sitting cross-legged, looking interested and pleased. Mrs Dunnitt had turned her head with an enquiring look towards Angel, who had struck one of her heroine-of-the-revolution poses and was glaring back at her.

"Finish," she snapped.

"I was just about to," said Mrs Dunnitt mildly.

"These lies, old woman. Finish now. Lies. Finish."

She strode forward, stuck out her arm and shoved Mrs Dunnitt hard in the chest with the flat of her palm. Mrs Dunnitt went sprawling. Mum gave a gasping cry and knelt beside her. Danny didn't move. While Mum was helping Mrs Dunnitt to a chair Angel stalked back to the spotlight.

She drew a deep breath. I could see she'd rehearsed what she was going to say—the way one does in a language one hardly knows—and had it all ready to burst out with.

"Now the court give deciding," she cried. "Deciding is . . ."

She stuck. She didn't know the word. The arm that wasn't holding the gun jabbed forward, thumb down. Slowly she swung it downwards, glaring at Mum as she did so. Mum turned, mouth open, towards her, and shook her head. Her spectacles had somehow got crooked on her face. She looked quite dazed.

"Now the court give punish," yelled Angel. "Punish is die."

Her beads rattled. The safety-catch clicked. The gun came slowly up to point towards Mum.

The children were screaming. I stood up and tried to get out of the pew but I got tangled with Mrs Slim who'd seen what was happening a moment earlier. I was still shoving desperately to get past her when I saw Chip striding up the centre aisle almost at a run. Instinctively knowing he'd cope I turned back to watch. Danny was watching too, relaxed on his chair, amused. I jumped to the idea that this was all part of his plan, the performance, but my heart went on banging like a sick machine. Mum had shrunk back against the pulpit. Angel was taking her time, but the gun was up and level when Chip arrived and gripped it by the barrel, pushing it down and to one side. Silence.

"No bullets," said Danny, smiling.

I felt the breath whoosh out of my lungs with sheer relief. Of course, I thought, it's only a play. They'd set it up. That's why they'd taken so long getting the table out of the porch, because they had to unload the gun . . . only they hadn't told Chip . . .

He was furious. He turned towards Danny. Angel wrenched at the gun. There was a colossal noise, so loud and near that I didn't understand that it was the gun actually firing. Everybody was yelling and screaming again. Danny was on his feet. Chip had let go of the gun with the shock but he grabbed it again just as Angel was swinging it up towards Mum. Two more shots banged before he wrenched it from her and turned towards Danny.

"You stupid jerk!" he yelled. "You know what she's like! She'd reloaded! You bloody stupid . . ."

Mum was staring amazed at her hand. It was a mess of scarlet. That was the last thing I saw before all the lights went out.

Glass crashed and tinkled. An enormous voice boomed from high up to one side.

"Down, everybody! Under the pews! Down! Down! Down!"

I dropped. Mrs Slim dropped on top of me, and I said "Sorry" as if I'd bumped into her on a crowded pavement. All round was thumping and scuffling, grunts, ouches and yells. I was only half on the floor and there was no room to get further so I heaved myself out from under Mrs Slim and lay along the seat of the pew. A foot kicked me in the eye. Three terrific bangs—I think it was three, but they were almost on top of each other—shook the church, so loud it was like being hit on the head and half-stunned. When my head cleared the lights were on again and the big voice was speaking Spanish.

It stopped and another voice, quite close, in the centre aisle, I thought, shouted, "Keep down everyone. All right, let's have you. One at a time. You first. Stay down! You, the big feller. Hands right up. Anyone else moves gets shot—got it? Now! March!"

Keeping my head on the pew seat but twisting my neck I saw Chip going down the centre aisle with his hands clasped on his scalp. Danny was next, then Angel. She hadn't got her hands up but her strange small head was stiff on its pillar of a neck and she was smiling. She was out of my sight when the voice said, "Hands up, you stupid bitch! Now out!"

There was a scuffle and a grunt, then footsteps moving away.

They kept us lying there for what seemed ages, though it can't have been more than a few minutes. I could see one window above the south aisle. The glass and wire were all smashed in and two shapes, black against the floodlights, poised there with guns. There'd be more at other windows, I realised—they'd have had something like this planned all along, but they couldn't risk it as long as one of the bandits was in the hide with his gun on us. It was only because Chip had had to come out to stop Angel . . .

At last the voice said, "Right, we'll have the rest of you out in a brace of shakes. No, stay down, please. First, anybody hurt?"

"Here," called Mrs Dunnitt.

"I'm all right," said Mum, but I could tell she wasn't.

"Let's have you then," said the voice. "Walk OK? Ambulance right outside, missus."

A moment later I saw Mum go past, leaning on Mrs Dunnitt's shoulder. Her left hand was wrapped in Mrs Dunnitt's grey cardigan but the blood was soaking through. Her face was grey and mauve. I thought, her left hand. Those sinewy muscles. Those fingers that know the Kodaly.

They took Juan next. From where I was I could only see the top of his head as he went past with one big soldier in front of him and another behind. Two minutes later I was staggering down the aisle, out into the dazzle of the floodlights, gulping in the road in Adam's arms. Mistily over his shoulder I saw the Mattean Embassy Rolls swing out of sight down Dryden Avenue.

"Where's Mum?" I managed to say.

"Hospital. Your Dad's gone with her in the ambulance."

Chapter Thirteen

In the end we managed two performances of the opera, a week late. I'll come back to that in a moment, but there's some tidying up to do first, though some of these bits happened before the performances and some after.

First Mum. It didn't seem nearly as bad as I'd been afraid. One of those last two shots, while Chip and Angel were fighting for the gun, had slashed across Mum's palm from side to side, mostly through that rubbery pad you have there and only chipping one tendon rather badly. The scar looks as though she'd picked up a bar of red-hot iron. The doctors said it should all heal and she'd be back playing in about six months. Nobody except her was hurt more than a few bruises, mostly got when we were cramming under the pews at the end.

They're going to try Danny and the other three of course, but it sounds as if it will take yonks before they get round to it. We've all been questioned and questioned, and besides that there are all the tapes the people outside took through their listening-bugs. Some of us will have to be witnesses but we don't know who they'll choose. The funny thing is that almost everyone I've talked to (except Mrs Banks) is terribly sympathetic to the bandits now, especially to Chip for stopping Angel shooting Mum. It's a pity that from one or two things various policemen have said it sounds as if he was the one who actually shot Ferdy. The children got together and sent a formal petition to the mafia asking for the profits from the opera to be sent to help the revolution in Matteo. There aren't going to be any profits

because of only having two performances, but in the circumstances that's a lucky break, as there'd have been a real row with the
toughies on the Church Council about using the money for that
instead of Onward's charities.

I suppose the children's attitude wasn't all that extraordinary.
I mean I know whose side I'm on now in Matteo, and I'm not
the only one. In fact Danny and his gang have got quite a bit of
what they were after, because since the siege there's been
absolutely endless TV coverage of affairs in Matteo, and
questions in Parliament, and features in the Sunday supplements,
and so on, all terrifically anti-Blick. Dad says our government is
pushing the Americans for a tougher line with the regime, for
instance getting Blick to announce some kind of amnesty for the
national holiday (which believe it or not is called O'Grady Day).
If he does, Adam says he still won't let anyone go who matters,
just a few hundred harmless bods who'd managed to get swept
up by the police machine, but even that would be something. (A
bit more than something, if you think about it.)

Naturally I couldn't talk about any of this when I took four of
the ravens to visit Ferdy in hospital. They'd chipped in to buy a tape
of the opera which they wanted to give him. Of course the mafia
would have let them have one free, but they really wanted to feel
they'd paid for it.

We could hardly recognise him. He was propped up in bed in
his own room in a private hospital in Swiss Cottage, but he was
thin and pale and his face so lined that he looked twenty years
older. He told us he'd been hit by five bullets, and he hinted that
he'd almost died twice. He swore he was getting stronger every
day but it wasn't easy to believe.

Anyway he was marvellously happy to see us. It turned out
that though his embassy was paying for his treatment he
practically never had any visitors. Katie Drew burst into tears
the moment she saw him and spent the whole visit having a
lovely weep. Ferdy was sweet with her and in fact it was almost
a relief to have her sniffling away, crying for all of us. We'd

brought along a tinny little cassette-player and I put on the raven
dance for him and he made a big effort and mimed playing the
guitar for it, but I could see he was tired by then so I took the
children away as soon as it was over.

When I got home I rang up Senora O'Grady, gulping with
nerves because I was sure she was going to bite my head off, but
she was pretty understanding in her ultra-grand way. She told
me she'd sent a message asking Ferdy whether he'd like to see
Juan, and Ferdy had been quite definite that he didn't want to. I
suppose he didn't mind us, because we'd only been Ferdy-fans
for a couple of months, but Juan had had him for a hero most of
his life, and now to let the kid see him lying there, smashed . . .
PDS or no, Ferdy was a decent bloke, and there's no getting
away from it.

I got in three more visits, alone, before they flew him home,
and I do think he was mending, but terribly slowly. I doubt if
he'll ever do his tiger-act again.

On my way back from that first visit I told Queenie Windsor I'd
like to come and talk to her mother. (I'd tried to put it over to
the mafia what she'd done, but they were so brimming with
everyone's doings that I never managed to make them grasp that
right at the beginning Queenie had pulled out something extra.)

"I'm afraid you can't," said Queenie in her solemn voice.
"Mum's left."

"Oh, I'm sorry."

"It's all right. She did it two years ago. Dad's got over it
now."

(Amazing, but typically Queenie.)

"Could I come and see him, then?"

"If you want to. Tonight's his Buddhist night but he won't be
doing anything tomorrow. Come about half-past eight."

I'd never seen Mr Windsor. He turned out to be a genuine
gnome, one of the bulgy sort with a pad of paunch squeezed in
by a thick leather belt, bald head, black beard, sparkling eyes,

and enormous pipe which squelched when he sucked it. His tobacco smelt like incense. He seemed to live in one basement room, as if he'd been a bachelor. There was a desk, a bed in one corner, cardboard boxes of books along the walls and piles of books all over the floor. No chairs, so we sat on huge cushions. He didn't feel like anybody's father. Perhaps that was why I made a better go of explaining what had happened in the back vestry than I had with the mafia.

"Thank you," he said at the end. "I'm glad to know that."

"I wanted to tell someone."

"Yes, I can see. And it's a help to me. She's had a few nightmares."

"I'm sorry."

"No, it's a relief. It shows she's human."

"I hate having nightmares."

"A bit of a Martian, Queenie. She needs the occasional nightmare."

He was perfectly polite, but creepy. We stopped talking about Queenie and got onto UFOs and ley-lines. He talked and talked and I pretended to listen while I tried to think out ways of arranging a bit more human contact for Queenie. But since then I've found out that she's terrifically popular at her school so I haven't worried.

Well, the opera. At first it didn't look as if we were going to be able to do it at all because the police insisted on hanging onto the church for days, measuring and photographing and so on—an utter waste of time when everyone knew what had happened. It was incredibly frustrating. But by the time the mafia had decided to cancel, pressure was building up to do it a week later. Families rang up and pleaded. The Lavers and the Farquson-Colquhouns both said they were going to cancel their skiing holidays rather than miss it. There was a sort of feeling that if we didn't put it on we'd be admitting that Danny had beaten us. Then the scaffold-hire firm rang up and said they wouldn't be charging any hire-fees and we could keep the scaffolding as long as we wanted, and Mr Tolland got the light-hire firm, who are usually foul about that sort of thing, to let us have the extra week free. And so on. In the end we decided to do two performances on the Saturday. We couldn't have the Sunday because that was the Church Nativity Play—nothing to do with the opera—and we're always terribly careful not to make it look as if we think the opera takes precedence.

Then the Talatis' phone never stopped ringing with utter strangers trying to buy tickets. We could have run for a fortnight if we'd wanted to. Luckily Mrs Talati's a total tough and made no bones about sorting out who could come and who couldn't, so in the end we weren't swamped by a lot of rubbernecks. It wasn't so easy with the tellymen. They were ghastly— far ghastlier in their own way than the two awful sound-recordists had been that other frightful year. They seemed literally incapable of grasping that having the TV cameras in and getting snippets of the opera on programmes like *Nationwide* wouldn't be the most marvellous thing that had ever happened to us. Even in a normal year the extra chaos wouldn't have made it worth while, and this year all we wanted to do was put the show on for ourselves and our families and our friends. It was private, but that isn't a word tellymen have in their dictionaries.

We said No, and No, and No, but on the very Saturday there was a camera crew trying to push their way in. The Talatis had organised a gang of extra helpers like Adam to cope with gate-crashers and there was almost a pitched battle, Adam told me, and one of the tellymen told him that he was an elitist parasite and Adam answered in the same language so that there was some fairly filthy dialectic flying around outside still when the show got started.

Late, as always. It was supposed to be 5.00 but it was almost 5.20. The church was packed, the cast crazy with excitement. I got my shoe-system working properly. Automatically I counted the ravens—seven, in through the west door, Juan into the usual bash-about with the twins. Right up to the last moment there'd been some doubt about whether the embassy would let him take part, but he got his way. He had a new guard, nothing like Ferdy, no help at all in keeping the little brutes in order.

That first performance went all right . . . at least the audience loved it and there were no real bloomers and it all sounded reasonable, but . . .

I suppose I was expecting too much, but as it went on I got drearier and drearier. I couldn't stop asking myself was it only for this that we did all that work and went through all that horror? Or had I changed? Had my mind lost its puppy-fat, grown up, put on a different kind of weight so that now I'd never be able to be whirled up again like a blown leaf in the storm of happiness that I'd taken for granted ever since I'd first put on that owl-mask and groped my way up the aisle squeaking *Kyrie Eleison*? I didn't know. When it was over I plodded through the hour-and-a-half between performances doing all my chores, snapping at anyone who got in my way, aching for the whole damn thing to be over.

Christmas stockings . . . Year after year Granny Jacobs said the same thing about them. If you don't expect anything, then you *might* find something in them. You mustn't spoil it by wanting or hoping. Perhaps that was why, at the second performance, it was different. I've listened to both tapes and I can't tell why now, but oh, at the time . . .

It was all my happiness over the years bundled into one hour and given back to me. It was that moment when the bonfire you've been coaxing and cosseting truly catches and turns from a smouldering heap all at once into a roaring glory, flames reaching up and up, warmth like the sun glowing out of the middle embers, faces lit with orange, grinning with triumph in the chill dusk. It wasn't only me. I knew that everyone felt the same. I was part of a shared glory that rang in the music, glittered in the lights, danced in every thread and muscle on the stage and burned through all our minds from Toby conducting on his podium to the smallest tribesman belting out the Yahweh shout. I did my bits in the dark without even thinking. My hands and feet knew what was needed while my mind joined in the triumph.

As it ended, and the audience whooped and cheered and the cast went wild and the orchestra improvised on bits and bobs of Bill's melodies and people like Mum (with her arm in a sling) and Mrs Dunnitt and Mrs Banks were dragged up onto the stage and given bouquets and things I watched from the font steps, in the dark, thinking "Marvellous. I've had my share. That's over, for ever." I didn't mind at all—it was true in any case because next autumn I'd be too busy cramming for Oxbridge and the winter after that, if all went well, I'd be up at Trinity and that's about as far as it's worth anyone my age looking into the future. But I wasn't only being practical. I felt I'd come to a definite changing-place and God, supposing He exists, had been kind enough to let me change on a high, with no regrets of any kind at all.

I explained to Adam about this during the thank-you party. There's always a cast-party first in the church, for the children —ice-cream and sausage rolls and lemonade, and all the brats rushing round and trying to rip the scenery to bits and throwing anything throwable at each other and doing monkey-tricks on the scaffolding. When that's over we do a preliminary clean-up and troop over to Mrs Banks's for the thank-you party. It gets more of a crush every year, with all the past helpers there, and all the people like me who are officially old enough to come, and all the kids who think they are too, and the orchestra sprawled on the sofas exchanging music-gossip, and teenagers learning how to get legless on cheap Italian wine, and the dads and mums swapping Square-chat, and Onward booming and beaming. I took Adam out onto the pavement for a bit of peace but that wasn't much better because Jake Laver and his cronies were testing each other's mopeds round the square though I doubt if half of them had licenses and no one was all that sober—God knows what would have happened if a policeman had been tactless enough to show up.

"You're dead lucky," said Adam when I'd told him.

"What do you mean?"

"Getting that much kick out of anything in the first place. Some poor bods it never happens to, not once in their lives. And then being able to pack it in and not try to hang on. That's as important as having it at all."

"Don't you rely on it. Some things I'm going to hang onto like grim death, and you're one of them."

"Exactly like grim death. I got a letter from Wadham this morning."

"You didn't! What? Are they . . . Why didn't you tell me before?"

"Waiting for your mind to clear. Anyway, they'll have me."

"That's amazing!"

"What do you mean amazing? I don't find it at all amazing."

"I mean terrific."

"Great place, Oxford. Lots of lovely brainy women around."

"Make the most of it. You're going to have exactly one year before I come up and sort them out for you."

He laughed and put his arm round me and led me back into the party.

I thought I'd finished writing this when I got to that line. I began in theory to practise touch-typing, but I suppose it's been useful to me in other ways. Anyway I'd got it all down and I was sorting through the manuscript last night when Trog came into my room. He's been staying for a couple of days because his firm's having a conference. At first he just mooned around in a troggish way, picking things up as though he expected to find beetles under them and putting them down again. It's a habit, but it usually means he's bothered about something.

Suddenly he said "What's this about Mum selling the Testori?"

"No!"

"She mentioned it in passing—what she was going to do with the money—sounded good as settled."

"First I've heard," I said.

(That wasn't surprising. Trog's always been closest to her.)

Trog looked for beetles in my oddment-box.

"Her hand seems perfectly all right to me," he said. "Apart from the scar, I mean. I made her let me feel it. You see I ran into Doctor Bissip at the Ramsays' last night. He says she ought to start playing again. It would be good for her hand."

"She was saying only last week she wasn't ready. Dad was getting at her to practise."

"You must tell him to stop that," said Trog sharply. "It's the worst thing he could do. I think this may turn out quite a serious problem, Dodo."

"Oh, please not! I couldn't bear it if she stopped playing!"

Trog opened a drawer and shut it again. He turned a pile of records over one by one and took some books out of the shelves and pushed them back. In the end he stood in the middle of the floor and scratched. He's been apt to do that since he was tiny. It doesn't mean anything. It's why he's called Trog.

"It isn't just the hand, is it?" he said. "That business in the church . . . I don't suppose that thug realised what he was doing, but it must have been a pretty effective kind of torture. We don't know anybody who's been physically tortured . . ."

(I do, but it wouldn't have helped to tell him.)

"She's changed," he said.

"I know."

"Tell me—the Testori—it imposes certain standards, doesn't it? Having an instrument like that, um? It could be a strain as you got older."

"Mum's not old."

"Suppose she were to flog it, and get something a bit less grand. Don't you think she might find it easier to come to terms with that?"

"She might . . . but I'd hate her to sell the Testori! I'd really hate it! It'd be giving in, don't you see? Almost like dying!"

Trog took off his shoe and stood on one leg peering into the darkness where the toes go.

"Even that—we're going to have to get used to the idea one day," he said.